KU-449-094

# Little Red Hen

by John McGrath

**fairplay press**

QUEEN MARGARET UNIVERSITY LRC

First published in 1977 by Pluto Press Ltd., Unit 10, Spencer Court, 7 Chalcot Road, London NW1 8LH.

This edition published by fairplay press, an imprint of Capercaillie Books Limited in 2008.

Registered office 1 Rutland Court, Edinburgh.

© John McGrath. The moral right of the author has been asserted.

Printed in the UK.

A catalogue record for this book is available from the British Library.

ISBN 978-1-906220-19-8

This book is sold subject to the condition that it shall not by way of trade or otherwise, be lent, resold, hired out or otherwise circulated without the publisher's prior consent in any form of binding or cover other than that in which it is published and without a similar condition including this condition being imposed on the subsequent purchaser. All rights reserved. No part of this publication may be reproduced, stored in a retrieval system or transmitted in any form or by any means, electronic, mechanical or otherwise without the written permission of the publisher. All applications for a licence to perform this play must be made before rehearsal to Casarotto Ramsay, Waverly House, 7–12 Noel Street, London W1F 8GQ. No performance may take place unless a licence has been obtained.

The publisher acknowledges support from the Scottish Arts Council towards the publication of this title.

**Scottish**
**Arts** Council

QUEEN MARGARET UNIVERSITY

100 202 085

$DP|11$

# Little Red Hen

John McGrath was born in Birkenhead, Cheshire, in 1935 from an Irish family. After education in Wales, national service and Oxford University, he wrote and directed for theatre and television, as well as writing for cinema. Early work included *Z-Cars* for BBC-TV (1962), *Events While Guarding the Bofors Gun* (1966) and the screenplay for *Billion Dollar Brain* (1967). In 1971, together with Elizabeth MacLennan, he co-founded the 7:84 Theatre Company, which divided into Scottish and English companies in 1973 with McGrath remaining as Artistic Director of both. During his career McGrath wrote over seventy plays, including *Fish in the Sea* (1972), *The Cheviot, the Stag and the Black, Black Oil* (1973), *Blood Red Roses* (1980), *Border Warfare* (1989), *Watching for Dolphins* (1992) and, most recently, *HyperLynx* (2001). He was twice Visiting Fellow in Theatre at Cambridge University. His previous books include *A Good Night Out* (1981), *The Bone Won't Break* (1990), *Six-Pack: Plays for Scotland* (1996), and *Naked Thoughts that Roam About* (2002) and *Plays For England* (2005).

McGrath founded Freeway Films in 1982, for which he produced, amongst others, *The Dressmaker* (1985), *Carrington* (1995), *Ma Vie en Rose* (1997) and *Aberdeen* (2002). He also founded Moonstone International Screen Labs to support and promote independent European filmmaking. He received Life-time Achievement Awards from both BAFTA (in 1993) and the Writers' Guild of Great Britain (in 1997), as well as Honorary Doctorates from the University of Stirling and the University of London. He died in 2002.

fairplay press

*If you remove the English tomorrow, and hoist the green flag over Dublin Castle, unless you set about the organisation of the Socialist Republic, your efforts would be in vain. England would still rule you. She would rule you through her capitalists, through her landlords, through her financiers, through the whole array of commercial and industrialist institutions she has planted in this country.*

**James Connolly, 1897**

# Introduction

7:84 Theatre Company was formed in 1971, with the aim of making theatre with socialist values for working-class audiences in England, Wales and Scotland. For the first two years we were based in London, and toured extensively, but in 1973 four of us who were Scots or had strong Scottish connections went off to start another company in Scotland, while the others carried on working in England and Wales.

The first production of the Scottish 7:84 was *The Cheviot, The Stag and the Black, Black Oil*, a show about the history of the Highlands. *Little Red Hen* was the sixth major production, which toured mostly in the industrial areas of Scotland from September to December 1975, also being performed subsequently in Ireland, and at the Shaw Theatre in London in June 1976.

Wherever we go in the industrial areas of Scotland – and Clydeside in particular – we meet up with an older generation of working-class militants who constantly astonish us. Active, articulate, passionate and well-informed, they draw their strength and conviction from the days of the 'Red Clyde' – days when the naked greed and ruthlessness of the capitalist system were plain to see; days when John MacLean, Jimmy Maxton, John Wheatley, Willie Gallacher and many other great activists and speakers expressed the demand of the Scottish working-class for the overthrow of capitalism and the creation of a socialist Scotland.

During the 1914–18 war, Glasgow was the centre of opposition to the senseless slaughter in the trenches, the exploitation of the workers in their factories to keep the slaughter going, and the rent-profiteers who owned their homes. After the war, in 1919, Glasgow workers lead the strike for a 40-hour working week to absorb the unemployed. There were 30,000 unemployed in Glasgow, and thousands more coming back from the trenches every week. On Bloody Friday, trouble flared up at a mass meeting in George Square. That night, the soldiers arrived and set up machine-guns on top of buildings in the city centre, and a howitzer in the City Chambers. The leaders were arrested. There was no violent revolution. But the anger, and the activism, continued. By 1922, the movement was so strong that ten out of the twelve Glasgow MPs returned at the election were socialists.

That generation saw Scotland on the move – in a big way. Today, we are told, Scotland is on the move again. The UCS work-in, the activism of the Scottish miners, the promised economic miracle of the oil industry, the up surge of nationalism – all point to an atmosphere at least of energy and debate.

In *Little Red Hen*, we try to take a look at that earlier time of high hopes, and at the present moment of aspiration, through the eyes of one of that older generation. What went wrong with the first period – which ended in the misery of the '30s – may be of interest to people today who are working, as she did, for a better future for the people of Scotland.

**John McGrath 1977**

# Characters

| | |
|---|---|
| YOUNG HEN | |
| OLD HEN: | her grandmother. |
| FREDDIE MULRINE: | OLD HEN's father. |
| NORA MULRINE: | her mother. |
| GEORGE MULRINE: | her brother. |
| CHARLIE: | her husband and political activist |
| J. RAMSAY MacDONALD: | M.P. and Prime Minister. |
| WILLIE GALLACHER: | an M.P. |
| JAMES MAXTON: | an M.P. |
| JOHN WHEATLEY: | an M.P. |
| DAVIE KIRKWOOD: | an M.P. |
| MRS CHARLOTTE SQUARE: | SNP politician. |
| HAMISH BANFF: | SNP politician. |
| WILLIAM McCASHIN: | SNP politician. |
| JOHN MacLEAN | |
| SUAVE YOUNG MAN | |
| LADY PARMOOR | |
| DUCHESS EUPHEMIA | |
| MRS BEATRICE WEBB | |
| LABOUR MP's WIFE | |
| SIR F. BANBURY | |
| DEPUTY SPEAKER | |
| KING GEORGE V | |
| BALDWIN | |
| WALTER CITRINE | |
| GENERAL THOMSON | |

ADMIRAL JELLIROLL

THE HON. DOUGALL

MINER

TUC

BUILDERS

POP GROUP

# Production Notes

## First Production

As presented by 7:84 Theatre Company (Scotland) in 1975.

| | |
|---|---|
| DAVE ANDERSON: | Composer/pianist; John Wheatley; Baldwin. |
| NADIA ARTHUR: | Costumes. |
| GINNI BARLOW:* | Mother (Nora Mulrine); Mrs Beatrice Webb. |
| JOHN BETT:** | James Maxton; Father (Freddie Mulrine); Suave Young Man. |
| WILMA DUNCAN:* | Young Hen. |
| FERI LEAN: | Administrator; Publicity. |
| JENNIFER LEE:** | Mother (Nora Mulrine); Mrs Beatrice Webb. |
| JOHN McGRATH: | Writer; Director. |
| DAVID MacLENNAN: | Lighting design; Company Manager. |
| ELIZABETH MacLENNAN: | Old Hen; Lady Parmoor; Accordion; Piano. |
| KRIS MISSELBROOK: | General Thompson; Deputy Speaker; Stage Manager. |
| TERRY NEASON: | Singer; Caddy; Duchess Euphemia; Guitar. |
| BILL PATERSON: | Harry Lauder; John MacLean; George Mulrine; J. Ramsay MacDonald. |
| BILL RIDDOCH: | Charlie; Willie Gallacher; Davie Kirkwood; Sir F. Banbury; Drums. |

| | |
|---|---|
| ALLAN ROSS: | Set design and construction; Fiddle; Mandolin; King George V; Admiral Jelliroll. |
| GINNI STARK:** | Young Hen. |
| FINLAY WELSH:* | James Maxton; Father (Freddie Mulrine); Suave Young Man. |

with the help of:

| | |
|---|---|
| JOHN BYRNE: | Poster design and set painting. |
| PAT LOVETT: | Choreography. |

\* first tour.

\*\* second tour.

## A Note on the Text

While 7:84 Theatre Company work as a collective, we do not write plays in committee. We try to use the special skills of individuals within the company to their best advantage, while still laying the results of those skills open to discussion and criticism. *Little Red Hen* is, therefore, my creation as a writer, reinforced by the contribution of the members of the company in rehearsal and in discussion. Dave Anderson, as the main tune-writer, contributed to the lyrics of some of the songs. Elizabeth MacLennan not only did a great deal of research, but also gave much to the character of the Old Hen. Bill Paterson's knowledge of Glasgow, Bill Riddoch's knowledge of the North-east of Scotland contributed greatly to their parts, and David MacLennan's research and arguments greatly affect sections of the play. The whole company poured in their thoughts, knowledge and enthusiasm in a way that makes working with them a great joy.

**John McGrath 1975**

# Act 1

As audience comes in, one or two quiet tunes from the musicians.

On stage, four plinths, with fronts painted as the top of Greek columns, of varying height. As the show progresses these plinths are used for the politicians, and turn, flap, extend, etc., to become armchairs, cupboards, etc. – in fact all the scenery needed for the show. At the back of the stage, against a sky-cloth, a large, painted cut-out of Glasgow tenements. Where possible, this is flown out and a large cut-out of the Palace of Westminster flown in for the whole London sequence in Act One.

Suddenly, an OFFICIAL VOICE comes over the speakers:

VOICE: Clear the stage now, come on, boys and girls – **(BAND disperse, shrugging.)** . . . Ladies and gentlemen – tonight, at your very own **(hall/club/theatre)** we are proud to bring to you – at immense cost to the tax payer, no expenditure spared, not one penny of the Scottish Arts Council's budget languishing unlavished, ladies and gentlemen – you asked for it, you're going to get it – at long last Seven: Eighty-four Theatre Company presents – HARRY LAUDER!

Blast of accordion music, and mock HARRY LAUDER appears, Och aye-ing, tells a few corny jokes and goes into a song. At chorus, all the COMPANY come on dressed identically as HARRY LAUDER and go through a Lauder routine of songs and dances, ending with *Keep Right on to the End of the Road*, then go, leaving the YOUNG HEN on stage. The overall impression is one of the old-style Tartan variety show, with yards of ersatz tartan, kilts, bonnets, etc., sentiment and joviality, climaxing in welter of emotion on the last number.

## Two hens

YOUNG HEN: Keep right on to the end of the road, eh? Aye, that's just what we're going to do, OK, keep right on to the end of the road until our own lovely Scotland's a nation once again: that's what I'm doing – and anybody who says any different should be dumped south of the border draped in a Union Jack, so they should. **(Sings)** *Flower of Scotland*, etc.

**A disturbance. OLD HEN waves her stick at her from audience.**

OLD HEN: Will yuh come down offa that platform and stop makin' a damn fool of yourself, Henrietta?

YOUNG HEN: Aw, Christ, it's ma Granny. See here, Granny, you go off and wave your red flag in Peking.

OLD HEN: Shut-your ignorant face, you're a disgrace to your grandfaither –

YOUNG HEN: What for? Jus' because I'm a patriot, a true Scot?

OLD HEN: Standin' there singing daft Harry Lauder songs, draped in yards of tartan like a Scottish Tourist Board rally –

YOUNG HEN: Don't you say one word against Harry Lauder, Granny, he may have been a bourgeois pig, but he was loved – and for why? Because he made Scotland famous all over the world.

**OLD HEN is clambering up on to the stage. She is a thin, dynamic old lady with a stick, and a Glasgow accent that harks back a few years.**

OLD HEN: He made the Scottish people look damn stupid all over the world.

YOUNG HEN: **(to audience)** I really don't know what the older generation's coming to, I do not. She's always been like that – they old people should be seen and not heard, that's what I say –

OLD HEN: Would you listen to that? Here's me been fighting for the labour movement in Scotland all my life, and her – the stupid baboon – tellin' me how she's gonnae make Scotland Free –

YOUNG HEN: So we will –

OLD HEN: Away and play wi' yoursel'.

YOUNG HEN: Granny! Would you no' be so obscene in front of these people? You're embarrassin' me.

OLD HEN: I don't give a damn for these people, I'm too far gone in my dotage to give a damn for anythin' but the truth.

YOUNG HEN: Aye, well. Could you just express it in a more kinda – acceptable manner?

OLD HEN: Away an' shite!

YOUNG HEN: You'll have to excuse her, she's gettin' past it – listen, Gran, I know you've had a fair scunner one way or another in your time, but we're not so stupid as you lot were – we know what we're doin'.

OLD HEN: Is that a fact?

YOUNG HEN: Aye! **(Sings)**
*Oh Flower of Scotland,*
*When will we see,*
*Your like again . . . ?*

OLD HEN: Would you listen to her? Well I'm tellin' you, young woman, you're no' showin' a glimmer of doin' anything of the kind.

YOUNG HEN: When Scotland's free – we're gonnae say how it's run.

OLD HEN: D'you think?

YOUNG HEN: I know.

OLD HEN: You've more chance of Bonnie Prince Charlie comin' back from the grave to claim his rightful throne – when Scotland's free. There's two Scotlands, hen, and don't you forget it – there's the Scotland that's you and me, that's been robbed and cheated and worked to the bone when it suits or thrown on the queue at the burroo when it doesnae suit – that's one Scotland; and there's a Scotland that owns factories like yours and sweat-shops like I worked in, and grouse moors and mountains and islands and stocks and shares, and says what goes – and there's only one of them can be free at a time – and don't you go kiddin' yourself it's going to be the workers –

YOUNG HEN: We're all gonnae be free.

OLD HEN: You know *nothin'*!

YOUNG HEN: Scotland's on the move, Gran.

OLD HEN: Aye, but do you know which way you're goin'? Or how you're gonnae get there? Do you buggery –

YOUNG HEN: Gran!

OLD HEN: I've seen something like it before, an' I'm for tellin' you about it – and listen tae what I'm tellin' you – for you'll need to remember – **(STAGE MANAGER comes on to remove tartan drapes.)** – Aye, you carry on, son, get rid of that rubbish – nineteen twenty-one. Scotland was on the move – and what was it we did then? Oh aye – it was the shimmy – Scotland, hen, was on the shimmy. **(Sings.)**

*Aw Jimmy*
*Come and dae the shimmy wimme*
*Gimme a shimmy or two*
*At the foxtrot I guess you're fine*
*But Jimmy when you're wimme it's*
*The shimmy for mine – ah luv it –*
*Aw Jimmy*
*Shake a shoulder, shake a shoulder*
*Take a guid haud a me, do – o,*
*Aw Jimmy when you're wimme,*
*Aw heaven forgimme*
*Ah could shimmy forever wi' you.*

Do you like that?

YOUNG HEN: Does Hughie Green know about you?

OLD HEN: Oh there's worse to come. The whole place was doin'
the shimmy – and I don't just mean in the dance-hall. The
industrial proletariat of Scotland was on the march – and by
God they had some great men to lead them – and they had
the right ideas – Jimmy Maxton, John MacLean, John
Wheatley, Willie Gallacher, Davie Kirkwood, Manny Shinwell –
well – could they speak? You had to hear it to believe it –
and, you *did* go to hear it – thousands went to hear it: and
the word they were speakin' was *socialism*. Not your wittery-
wattery buggered-up capitalism with knobs on you get now
– the real thing.

Come away and hear them at it –

**Light comes up on WILLIE GALLACHER standing on plinth.**

GALLACHER: My name is Willie Gallacher from Paisley, and I've
dedicated my whole life to the overthrow of capitalism. I've
been an industrial militant ever since I started working for a
rat of a greengrocer. I was Glasgow's first twelve-year-old
shop-steward.

In nineteen nineteen I stowed on board a boat for Norway, and made my way to Moscow. When I met Lenin, he informed me I was too left-wing for him. So I was. All the same, he asked me to go back and help create the Communist Party of Great Britain – which I did. I believe there is only one way for the working people of this country to end the exploitation of their labour, and their lives, and that is to seize state power, retain it, and establish the dictatorship of the proletariat as a means of transition to a communist society. I will go to prison for believing that, I will suffer for it, but I shall die still firm to that belief and still working to bring it about.

YOUNG HEN: Hey, wait a minute, Gran, that fella's a communist.

OLD HEN: So he was. An' if you think he was a wee bit red, you wait till you hear this one.

**Light comes up on JOHN MacLEAN on next plinth.**

MacLEAN: My name is John MacLean from Pollokshaws. The monstrous war we have lived through shows that the day of social pottering or 'reform' is past. The 'social reformer' must be absolutely crushed, for intolerance to him is but justice to humanity. However Labour may attain power, it must do as the Bolsheviks are doing. It must get full possession of land and all means of production in order to use these co-operatively by the whole community for the advantage of all.

I stand four square for the ending of capitalism – in Scotland, as elsewhere in the world – and the establishment of the Scottish Workers Republic in which alone, we in Scotland can achieve true independence.

YOUNG HEN: That's the man that says what I say, good on you – what was his name?

OLD HEN: John MacLean.

**Light goes up on JAMES MAXTON.**

MAXTON: My name is James Maxton, also from Pollokshaws. I'm a member of the ILP, I believe in Home Rule for Scotland, and I believe in socialism. Of course, for believing that, Calton Jail was for a spell my ancestral home. Labour must fight and fight to win! To win socialism in our time. The pathway of reformism or gradualism does not do for me when I see the children of Bridgeton going to school with a careworn look, when only joy and play should be in their minds.

It is all very well to say that we must build 'brick by brick' a structure of socialism – but you've got to get the bricks, and they are in the hands of capitalists. And even if you get the materials to build your edifice, you get it on capitalist conditions. In the end you find you have built not the Palace of Socialist Freedom, but a slum dwelling for the working classes.

We place our faith in the common working people of our land, inspired with courage, hope and determination, to build the new Society.

OLD HEN: Good old Jimmy – what a speaker, eh? You don't see the likes of that on your telly in between Robert Mackenzie and the bloody swingometer, do you my darlin'?

YOUNG HEN: Who's that one?

**Light goes up on JOHN WHEATLEY.**

WHEATLEY: My name's John Wheatley, from Shettleston, and I'm a Pape; mind you, the Pope's no' very fond of me because I let it be known that I thought his encyclical on the rights of workers to respect private property and to do as they're told was a load of papal bull. I've stood on my own doorstep and watched two thousand drunk Catholics burning my effigy on the pavement. It was quite a good likeness.

I started my working life as a miner, ten years down the pit, then I got a job selling advertising space for the Catholic press. Then I had a great idea – free holy blotters, with a wee message from the clergy: and all around the edge – adverts. Valuable space. I cleaned up. Now I've got a small printing and publishing business of my own. Aye, well, it works out useful in the struggle. What's the struggle for?

A Labour majority in parliament to take over the land, take over the mines, establish socialism now, and end the criminal exploitation of man by his fellow man – that's what the struggle's for, and we are going to win. Don't be deceived by my diffident manner, comrades. I bloody mean it.

OLD HEN: That was the clever one, that Wheatley. He couldnae help being a Pape; but it did stop him gettin' to grips with Karl Marx, and that was his downfall.

YOUNG HEN: And was they all in the Labour Party?

ALL: No we were not!

GALLACHER: Now when I met Lenin, he said to me –

MacLEAN: Don't listen to him – ever since he sneaked into the Kremlin he thinks he's Lenin's gramophone – seventy-eight revolutions per minute.

GALLACHER: Unfortunately my good friend MacLean here had went mental round about this time.

MAXTON: I have the greatest respect for these two gentlemen – mental or otherwise – but they tend to scare most people out of their wits, and if you're going to win an election, you need most people.

WHEATLEY: There's enough to be done round here without arguing amongst ourselves. So let's get down off these soap-boxes and away and do something.

ALL: Right.

**They all go off, JOHN MacLEAN alone, WHEATLEY and GALLACHER arguing, JAMES MAXTON whistling.**

OLD HEN: What a bunch! – And there was others, just as good. It was a great time to be alive and in Scotland. Apart from the poverty, the unemployment, the rickets, the TB and the beasts in the head.

YOUNG HEN: So which one of that crowd were you shouting for?

OLD HEN: Me? Oh, I couldn't give a damn about politics – till this particular night – I mind it well – it was just after tea time and there was five of us all squeezed into this room and kitchen. Ach, wait a minute – I'll show you. Make as if you're me – **(Hands her a shawl and long skirt.)**

YOUNG HEN: Me? Be you? What do I dae?

OLD HEN: Get oot o' that daft Japanese tartan, and into these.

## The lower depths of Bridgeton

**OLD HEN goes up stage and yells to the company, who come on to listen.**

OLD HEN Come on, you lot. Dae something for your living. Create – the Lower Depths of Bridgeton – well, shake a bloody leg.

**As the COMPANY set up the MULRINE family interior, a kitchen, with curtained bed recess and two armchairs, a sink and food shelves, OLD HEN talks to the audience.**

OLD HEN: They're supposed to be bloody actors, this lot, and they spend half their time singin' an' the other half drinkin'. I bet there's half of them no' paid up their Equity dues. **(To COMPANY.)** Now I want some proper actin', d'you hear? There's proper theatre-goers and theatre critics and God knows what else paid good money to see you, so none of your cheap satirical rubbish – d'you hear me? Are you right? **(Calls FIDDLER.)** Hey you, big fella, put down that can and set the mood with some suitable music . . . **(FIDDLER agrees, plays quiet tune.)**

YOUNG HEN: What do I do?

OLD HEN: Just sit down there, and think about fellas . . .

YOUNG HEN: Big fellas, little fellas, or what?

OLD HEN: Suit yoursel'. They're a' the same whatever shape they come in. Now here's your brother George. He was in the war, was George, and now he doesnae say anything.

YOUNG HEN: Nothin' at all?

OLD HEN: Well, he's no just a dummy, you know, but he was awf'y quiet. He's makin' a jumpin' jack for your wee sister Agnes. There's your mother worrying herself stupid about Agnes – so were we all. And – oh God, here's your faither comin' and he's got somebody wi' him.

**Gestures to FIDDLER to desist, which he does quietly. She watches as FATHER and CHARLIE come on, arguing about football. They come to the door.**

FATHER: Will you no' come in for a wee minute, Charlie?

CHARLIE: No – no – no, I'll go on up the stairs – I'm taking round these wee pamphlets for the election, you know – here, there's one for you, see an' you come to the meetin'. I'll distribute these to the folk up the stair.

FATHER: What's this for?

CHARLIE: It's tellin' you to get out and vote for Jimmy Maxton, which I hope you do anyway, and its tellin' you there's a few meetings you should be getting along to, right?

FATHER: Meeting? Votin'? Here, take it, don't waste your good pamphlet on me – I don't vote. Nor do I go to meetings.

CHARLIE: How no'?

FATHER: It's no' for the likes of me.

CHARLIE: That's just who it *is* for – the likes of you and the likes of me. Christ, – if you've never even voted, it's about time you did –

FATHER: **(awkward)** No, no – no, no.

CHARLIE: Well just read it, won't you, Freddie, it's for you.

FATHER: Well, I'll take one in wi' me, eh?

CHARLIE: See that – 'Housing: We in the ILP refuse to accept the appalling conditions in which the working class is forced to live. Here in Bridgeton alone . . .'

FATHER: Charlie – can you no' see? I cannae read.

CHARLIE: Oh. Well – that's nothin' to be ashamed of, Freddie. Here – is that how you've never voted?

FATHER: Aye. I wouldnae know what to do. But I'll give one to the girl – she likes readin'.

CHARLIE: Do you want to vote?

FATHER: Well, I suppose I should.

CHARLIE: And if you did – who'd you vote for?

FATHER: Well it'd no' be the Tory, I'm no' that stupid.

CHARLIE: And Nora?

FATHER: Och, she's worrit senseless wi' the wain, she'll no' be wantin' to go votin' or nothing like that.

CHARLIE: And what about George?

FATHER: No. He'll no' shift. It's three years since he came back, but the war's just finished him off. He's no' daft or shell-shocked or anythin' – but he'll no' vote. It's too much like speakin'.

CHARLIE: Maybe I will come in then for a wee minute . . .

FATHER: Will ye? Aye. Come on then, son.

**They go in to the small area of the room. GEORGE gets his jumping jack to work, and shows it proudly.**

MOTHER: Oh, here, that's great. **(To AGNES, who is behind curtains.)** Here, Agnes, see what George's made for you – look at it, is it no' good? **(To FATHER.)** Aw God, Freddie, she'll no' even raise her eyes to look at it, poor wee thing.

FATHER: Is she no' better?

MOTHER: Well, I wouldnae say she's worse, but she's no' exactly better – it's this bloody room, the walls is wringing wet and she cannae get air to breathe at all. **(To CHARLIE.)** Hello, Charlie.

CHARLIE: Aye, Nora. I'm sorry about the wain.

MOTHER: She's no' right.

FATHER: Here, girl – **(To YOUNG HEN.)** – somethin' tae read.

YOUNG HEN: Oh – what is it?

FATHER: Meeting – votin': Charlie's – er . . .

CHARLIE: Look, I'm sorry to bother you at a time like this wi' sickness in the family, but I'm bound to say, I find it incredible that wi' the situation you're in, there's not one of you going out to vote for the one man who's likely to try an' make things better for you.

YOUNG HEN: Jimmy Maxton, do you mean?

CHARLIE: I do, hen. There's folk fightin' in the trade unions for better wages for us and decent hours and better conditions and you're supportin' *them* I hope . . . no?

FATHER: They trade unions is trouble.

CHARLIE: You'll no' get anything without a bit of trouble, Freddie. But what we need now is Maxton and his colleagues to get up there into parliament an' tell them fools in London we're no' standin' for it any more.

**Silence.**

CHARLIE: Look, missus, you've said it yourself. These old houses are no' fit to be lived in the way they are — no wonder yer bairn's sick, no wonder she's no' gettin' better — now I'm not sayin' 'Get out and vote for Maxton and you're gonnae get three months' holiday on the French Riviera', no, but what I am saying is if us and the likes of us don't vote for him and the likes of him, this tenement's still going to be standing here in fifty years' time, still wringin' wet, still stuffed full of sick bairns and underpaid, overworked people. For why? Because the place is owned by a landlord — right? Now what does that mean . . . ?

**He carries on as OLD HEN speaks over.**

OLD HEN: Could that boy argue? He made George Bernard Shaw sound like Basil Brush. I sat mesmerised: a whole new side of life I'd never even knew existed – and a whole new side of Charlie Sullivan I'd never even knew existed.

FATHER: See, Charlie, old Fairlie that owns this house – right? Well – he's paid for it. Out of his own money. So it's *his*. Right? Am I right or am I wrong?

CHARLIE: Oh, God, Freddie, you're under the thumb of the system.

FATHER: Oh – wait a minute – no – I'm wrong. Now Charlie's gonnae tell me where I'm wrong. Fella buys somethin' out his own pocket – but it's no' *his*. Come on now, Charlie, tell me where I've gone wrong.

CHARLIE: Right, well – whose house are we in now – yours or mine?

FATHER: Mine – no – his. Like – I'm livin' in it, but it's his. If he doesnae want me livin' in it – oot. He throws me oot. That's the story.

CHARLIE: Right. Now I go and buy a knife, a very sharp knife – I pay for it out of my own money, out of my own pocket – so it's mine. And I think – that's a good wee knife that, I wonder if it would cut a finger off. So I go in the pub – go up to somebody – a total stranger – and I cut his finger off. What's wrong wi' that?

FATHER: It's no' your finger.

CHARLIE: No, but it's my knife. And if your landlord can throw you out because it's his house, how can I no' cut your finger off with my knife? It's no my finger – but it's no' the landlord's wife and wains'd be on the street: that man'll be doin' you a hell of a sight more actual grievous bodily harm throwin' you on the street than I would be cutting your finger off, but what he does is legal – sanctified in the law of the land. Well, that law's gonnae change – when Jimmy Maxton gets enough votes.

MOTHER: **(comes in from bed recess, worried.)** Here, I'm away to get the doctor: that wain's no gonnae last till momin' . . . I think you'd better have your argument somewhere else . . .

CHARLIE: Oh, I'm sorry, Nora – am I disturbing her?

MOTHER: That's alright, Charlie. If what you say is right, Charlie, and this man's gonnae speak up for us, you're quite right to do what you're doin'. But he's no' gonnae be in time to help that one. It's a doctor she's needing, no' a politician. **(She goes out.)**

CHARLIE: I'll go.

FATHER: Maybe you'd better, Charlie. **(As CHARLIE goes, FATHER stops him.)** Er . . . I'll vote for the man.

CHARLIE: Right. Cheerio. I hope – aye, well. **(Goes.)**

**Silence.**

FATHER: Well, George?

GEORGE: **(clears his throat uneasily.)** They're a' the same.

FATHER: Oh Christ. Charlie's away an' left his wee pamphlets . . .

YOUNG HEN: **(to OLD HEN.)** What do I do now?

OLD HEN: Put on your skates and deliver the bloody things tae every house in the close and every close in the street – that's what you do . . .

**Music in, as YOUNG HEN takes pamphlets and goes.**

OLD HEN: That was the day I joined the ILP.

**SINGER sings *Red Hen* song:**

> *Little hen goes running round*
> *From street to street*
> *Doing what there is to do –*
>
> *Little hen goes running round*
> *She's found her feet*
> *Nothing's going to stop her*
> *Till the job is through . . .*

**Music continues.**

OLD HEN: **(Speaks over.)** Christ, did I work – well, the job was there to be done, and a' my life – if there was something needin' daein', I'd just get up an' dae it – pamphlets? Leaflets? I've delivered millions of them from that day to this; chalking out the streets for the speakers, putting out the chairs in the halls, sweeping the bloody halls, makin' the tea, addressin' envelopes, shifting jumble: well, I was nae good at arguin' or speakin' – but that was what I could dae, so I did it.

**Song up again.**

> *Planting little seeds to grow one day*
> *Grow up into fields of wheat*
> *Little Red Hen, like the story books say*
> *Works so one day we can eat.*
> *Little hen gives all her strength*
> *To win that fight.*
> *Seems her strength is never done*
> *Little hen gives all she has*
> *She knows she's right*
> *Nothing's going to stop her*
> *Till the fight is won.*

**During the last part of the song, YOUNG HEN goes back into the room, in her character as the YOUNG OLD HEN, worn out. CHARLIE comes in, and persuades her to set off again with more pamphlets. As the song ends she comes back on to OLD HEN as herself.**

## Victory and off to Westminster

YOUNG HEN: Did yous win?

OLD HEN: We battered them – They Tories in the Western Club must have thought the world had come to a full stop. Out of twelve seats in Glasgow – the ILP won ten. Fair enough, the Tories won the election, but we won Glasgow. Nineteen twenty-two was the year the Red Clyde reached its parliamentary apotheosis –

YOUNG HEN: You what?

OLD HEN; And demonstrations? Aw, you missed yoursel' – you bourgeois nationalists thought you had a bit of a send-off for Winnie Ewing when she got in – eh?

YOUNG HEN: Aye, it was great – I was there.

OLD HEN: Nuthin'. St Andrews Halls were packed to the rafters the night before they went. They pledged theirselves to do God knows what; we sang the Hundred and Twenty-fourth Psalm, we sang the Twenty-third Psalm, Neil MacLean announced the old parliamentary order was finished, Manny Shinwell was wondering just how they could possibly live up to it all, and Jimmy Maxton got up to speak. There was silence.

**During this speech the room set is transformed back into plinths.**

YOUNG HEN: Did he forget his speech?

OLD HEN: Shut up! You wee besom.

**MAXTON gets up on to a plinth.**

MAXTON: Comrades and friends: we who are going off to Westminster do not go as so many individuals to win glory for ourselves. We go as a team – a team working towards one goal – and that goal is the abolition of poverty. There is some talk – there are some people talking – in a worried kind of a way – about the 'atmosphere' of the House of Commons getting the better of us wild men from the Clyde. Comrades – I've got news for them: the atmosphere of the Clyde is going to get the better of the House of Commons.

**CROWD sing 23rd Psalm.**

OLD HEN: And there was such a shout and cheers and the next night there was at least one hundred thousand people in St Enoch Square to see them off – where's your Winnie Ewing the noo?

**In background, *Red Flag* takes over from 23rd Psalm. WHEATLEY, with overcoat and case, comes on.**

WHEATLEY: Until this day, in my practical politics as a Baillie and a member of the Glasgow Corporation, I have been a cautious man. I have acted on the principle that we, as socialists, must not go too far ahead of what the mass of the people want. When I see these streets lined with people, when I see the square in front of the station jammed tight with over one hundred thousand citizens madly enthusiastic, not for the MPs themselves, but for the socialism for which they stood, I know I was wrong. It is being proven to me, at this minute, beyond doubt, that the people are ready to respond to a bold socialist lead.

**Red Flag ends.**

YOUNG HEN: So: what happened?

OLD HEN: So what happened – they got on the train.

**MAXTON and WHEATLEY, with their suitcases, get on to the train – two stools side by side facing the audience. The BAND starts a slow train rhythm, that speeds up as MAXTON and WHEATLEY, excited and determined, sit discussing what they are going to have to do at Westminster. As the rhythm works up to full speed, WHEATLEY jumps up and starts to sing a mock 'tough' number –**

WHEATLEY: *We're gonna shake Westminster*
*till its bells start to ring –*
*Gonna make a hell of a noise –*

**MAXTON jumps up and joins in:**

MAXTON/WHEATLEY: **(together)**
*Gonna make them sorry that they started this thing –*

WHEATLEY: Right, Jim?

MAXTON: Right, boys –

WHEATLEY: *We're gonna raise the Red Flag over*
*Ten Downing Street,*
*Gonna throw King George on the burroo –*

MAXTON/WHEATLEY: **(together)**
*Gonna agitate until the Soviets meet –*

WHEATLEY: Right, Jim?

MAXTON: Too true –

**SINGERS join in as the BAND gets up steam – and MAXTON and WHEATLEY sleep uncomfortably.**

SINGERS: *Night-train –*
  *Through the unknown places*
  *Leaving –*
  *What they knew,*
  *Far from –*
  *Those familiar faces –*

MAXTON/WHEATLEY: **(jumping up from sleep)** Do we have to change our train at Crewe?

SINGERS: *Cruising*
  *Through the English Country*
  *Things go –*
  *Bump in the night*
  *Strange sounds*
  *On the English platform –*

WHEATLEY: Wake, Jim?

MAXTON: Too right . . .

**Train starts to slow down.**

WHEATLEY: *Feeling kind of homesick and we haven't arrived*
  *Feeling kind of tired and low –*

WHEATLEY/MAXTON: **(together)**
  *Feeling unconnected wanting back to the Clyde –*

SINGERS: *Euston!*

MAXTON/WHEATLEY: **(together)**
  *Euston?*

SINGERS: *Euston*!

MAXTON/WHEATLEY: **(together)**
  *Oh no . . .*

**MAXTON and WHEATLEY doze off again. The skyline of Glasgow drops down and the Houses of Parliament arise in sunny splendour.**

**A figure in frock-coat appears tentatively behind them: J. RAMSAY MacDONALD. He looks at them, and then addresses the audience over their heads, in rhyming couplets, with occasional asides in prose.**

MacDONALD: J. Ramsay MacDonald speaking
  A great parliamentary career's what I'm seeking:
  I may look like a bit of a smarty
  But in fact I'm in the Labour Party.

  When they say that my politics are soft
  I remind them – I was born in a croft
  And though I now hob-nob with grand lords
  I once fearlessly criticised the landlords.

  **(Confidentially)** In a preface to a book, as a matter of fact; of course that was in nineteen hundred and five, and some long time ago, but a little reputation for being red goes quite a long way in the Labour party; damned useful, too.

  Now this man Clynes is a boring wee bleeder
  It's time I'd a shot at being Labour leader –
  But alas and alack, woe betide!
  I'm in need of the votes of these wild men from the Clyde –
  I'll stand in a good left-wing stance **(Poses.)**
  Then maybe I'll stand a bit of a chance –

  So watch this: I think you'll be impressed –

  **(To MAXTON and WHEATLEY, using mock Glasgow accent.)** Hullo rare Jimmies, we's – eh – ah – we's are gonnae have a wee bit vote an' that, for leader, if ya follow me, boys – see what I mean – it's like, well, see that fella Clynes – well – it's either him or me. So who're you voting for?

MAXTON: Clynes?

WHEATLEY: Or you?

MAXTON/WHEATLEY: **(together)** We abstain.

MacDONALD: Oh, come on now – don't forget, I'm your boy – I'm dead Red. I am a big wheel in the ILP – Surely you boys are going to vote for me?

MAXTON/WHEATLEY: **(together)** We'll think about it . . .

MacDONALD: Good – Then at this point I will be gone. You'll be seeing more of me anon. **(Pauses.)** I'm going to exit left: I think that's significant. Of course, it won't look left to you. It'll actually look right to you. But if it looks right to you, I'm satisfied.

**He goes. WHEATLEY looks at MAXTON.**

MAXTON: Clynes or MacDonald? John – what have we done?

WHEATLEY: We have joined his Majesty's loyal Opposition . . .

**They pick up their cases and go. Music immediately begins, and the set changes to smart London interior – a party given by wealthy Labour supporters.**

## Cocktails

**GENERAL THOMPSON, ADMIRAL JELLIROLL, LADY PARMOOR, DUCHESS EUPHEMIA, J. RAMSAY MacDONALD, MRS BEATRICE WEBB, SUAVE YOUNG MAN and THE HON. DOUGALL come on with drinks.**

SUAVE YOUNG MAN: **(comes and chatters excitedly to the audience.)**. We think they're going to be awfully droll – haven't you heard? They're going to be fascinating – in an appalling sort of way: we're getting fifty-six brand new Labour MPs – all to ourselves – one simply can't wait. Lancashire lads, doubtless in clogs, with all the latest scandals from Heckmondwyke – what a laugh: tiny Welsh miners with their Davy lamps to lighten our darkness; the girls are agog, one hears; gruff Yorkshire terriers, chattering tales of muck and brass; in Bradford – I think that's in Yorkshire; and the Scotties, oh, there's a thrill, in kilts, with claymores, skirling away on their bagpipes – muttering strange incomprehensible sounds about Lenin, and bloody revolution. And all of them, all of them – well, nearly all of them – breathing fire – one simply longs to see them.

**At the end of song, J. RAMSAY MacDONALD breaks away and, as music continues languidly on piano:**

MacDONALD: All those wild men roaring down from the Clyde
And Wales and the North and God knows where beside
Are turning my party into a fearsome scrimmage
They're common, uncouth and spoiling our image.
For Government's high oflioe we must seem to be fit –
But how can that be when they belch and scratch and spit
The people who matter will soon make a mockery
Of their Welshity, Northernness and unspeakable Jockery
Now I'm the leader I shall make it my job
To teach them. good manners, to curtsey and bob
A party of workers is obviously rejectable
I shall make it my business to make them eminently respectable.

**As J. RAMSAY MacDONALD ends, ALL advance on audience and sing.**

ALL: *Going to Westminster's rip-ping fun*
  *Now you've won*
  *It's better than Shettleston*
  *But for a chap to get on a bit*
  *One must take one's cocktails –*

**LADY PARMOOR goes over and accosts WHEATLEY.**

LADY PARMOOR: Ah, Mr Wheatley . . .

WHEATLEY: Yes, Lady Parmoor, what can I do for you?

LADY PARMOOR: I find it distressing that so far as I know I have not had the pleasure of meeting *Mrs* Wheatley – I was asking myself whether she might not care to drop in on one of my Tuesday luncheon parties? She'd meet some frightfully keen people . . .

WHEATLEY: Mrs Wheatley prefers to live in Glasgow.

LADY PARMOOR: Oh, Oh, how amusing . . .

WHEATLEY: And besides, Tuesdays is wash day.

**Music up. LADY PARMOOR goes of laughing wildly. ALL sing.**

ALL: *Living in London is Oh So Sweet*
  *Quite a treat*
  *It's better than Rutherglen*
  *But to be wholly acceptable*
  *One must have good manners.*

**Music goes on, DUCHESS EUPHEMIA chats to MRS BEATRICE WEBB.**

DUCHESS EUPHEMIA: My dear, d'you know the other day I was fascinated to read that the wife of your Deputy Leader – what's his name? Sounded Jewish – ah yes, Clynes – that

Mrs Clynes believes the time is ripe for the daughters of Labour leaders to be presented at Court – whatever next – socialist debutantes . . .

MRS BEATRICE WEBB: And why not, pray – there's nothing inferior about socialists . . .

DUCHESS EUPHEMIA: The season will never be the same – lawks a mussy – champagne and pigs' trotters . . .

**Music comes up as ALL sing next bit of song.**

ALL: *Be a sport and join in the game*
*Life's too short, too boring and tame*
*Don't be liverish and so working-class*
*Speak our gibberish, or you'll end up on your arse –*

*– Ha ha-ha, Ha ha-ha –*

*Going to Westminster's rip-ping fun*
*Now you've won*
*It's better than Dennistoun*
*But for a chap to get on a bit*
*One must show good, breeding.*

**A LANCASHIRE LABOUR MP's WIFE appears, smiling coyly. She commits a social blunder, then is lead forward.**

LABOUR MP's WIFE: I have lived all my life among the cotton mills of Lancashire. Now my husband is in parliament, I can safely say I have achieved my life's ambition. I have met Her Majesty the Queen. And she is a Very Gracious Person.

**Music swells up. WHEATLEY, MAXTON and KIRKWOOD walk into the party – squeals of delight, etc. ALL sing except them.**

ALL: *What a treat, some Labour MPs*
*They're so sweet, so easy to please.*
*Though they may be rough, they're the craze today*
*When we've had enough, we can send them all away.*

**Music continues as KIRKWOOD speaks to a circle.**

KIRKWOOD: See, ah'd just got up and made this speech, about the desperate conditions of the crofters in the Outer Hebrides. The Tories listened in silence – then voted to do nothing about it. As I was leaving the House of Commons, this Tory MP comes up to me – Mr Kirkwood? he says. Aye, Davie Kirkwood here. Mr Kirkwood, I could not vote for you but I should like to help these people if I may. Here – take this five pound note.

**WHEATLEY and MAXTON exchange glances and go away from group in general direction of the piano. KIRKWOOD is buttonholed by MRS BEATRICE WEBB.**

MRS BEATRICE WEBB: Tell me, Mr Kirkwood, what do you think of our parliament?

KIRKWOOD: Well, to speak the truth to you, Mrs Webb – or should I not say Lady Pasfield?

MRS BEATRICE WEBB: No, no. We're Fabians, we don't use the title: call me Beatrice.

KIRKWOOD: That's just an example of what I was going to say: before I entered the House of Commons, I'm afraid I knew little of the Great Ones, the Powerful Ones, the Lordly Ones; by the way, you can read all this in my autobiography – My Life of Revolt – but when I entered the House I found it was full of wonder. I had to shake myself occasionally as I found myself walking about and talking with men whose names

were household words. More strange was it to find them all
so simple, unaffected and friendly.

**Sighs of relief and content all round, as tune comes in again.
ALL sing.**

ALL: *The life of a gentleman's frightfully nice*
*Don't think twice*
*It's better than navvying –*

KIRKWOOD: **(solo)** *Choose the right friends, in a year or two –*
*You can join the peerage*

ALL: *Be a sport and join in the game*
*Life's too short, too boring and tame*
*Don't be liverish and so working-class*
*Speak our gibberish or you'll end up on your arse.*
*Going to Westminster's awful fun*
*Now you've won*
*It's better than Shettleston*
*But for a chap to get on a bit*
*One must take one's cocktails.*

**ALL sweep off laughing and braying with confidence.**

## Hard words at Westminster

**Enter YOUNG HEN and OLD HEN, dismantling cocktail party
set.**

YOUNG HEN: There y'are, you see – jus' what do you expect?
Let decent, honest people go down to London and they'll
turn into monkeys on sticks. What I say is – they should have
stayed here where we can keep an eye on them.

OLD HEN: Ye're talking rubbish – you couldnae even keep an
eye on the Glasgow Corporation – and that's just up the street.

YOUNG HEN: Its no' rubbish. That's why I say we should have our own parliament, right here in Scotland.

OLD HEN: Aye, but don't you see, hen, it's no' so simple – it was the bourgeois parliament itself that buggered them up. Listen to that David Kirkwood, him that was working at Parkhead Forge wi' the arse out of his breeks – 'how strange to find them all so bloody friendly'. Naw, it was no' so strange, Davie. They were after you, boy, they needed you, and by Christ they got you.

YOUNG HEN: And did they all end up like him?

OLD HEN: No, hen. Jimmy Maxton and John Wheatley took a fair scunner to the whole Westminster wonderland, and Maxton thought he was going to get a hold of the House of Commons and shake it till its bells rang – give him his due – he went at it like he said he would. **(Scene is changing to House of Commons. On comes DEPUTY SPEAKER, MAXTON, WHEATLEY, SIR F. BANBURY, etc.)** It was this hot June afternoon. Our parliament was discussing public health in Scotland – viz, they were taking away the milk from sick babies. Some Tory doctor MP from Dumfries arose to say how people didnae need health anyway. There was a couple of Tories too geriatric to move out, and a few of the Clyde men were waiting and watching. At six o'clock Jimmy got up to speak to a deserted House.

MAXTON: I have listened to the speeches of the Under Secretary of State and of the Hon. Member for Dumfries with some considerable impatience, because I feel that both of them have been doing their very best to soothe the public conscience on a matter in regard to which the public consciences has no right to be at ease.

I gather from the report that in Scotland last year there were twelve thousand, four hundred and seventy-two cases of tuberculosis notified.

There is some division of opinion as to the causes of this disease; there is much division of opinion as to treatment and possibilities of cure: but it is admitted by all that sunlight is an important element; and that good, nutritious, wholesome food is also an element, both in preventing the disease and in effecting a cure.

In another part of the Report, we find the statistic dealing with the poorhouses of Scotland. To maintain an average man, his wife and four children in the Barnhill Poorhouse costs fifty-eight and sevenpence, ha'penny per week. In the City of Glasgow there are few skilled artisans *getting* fifty-eight and sevenpence ha'penny a week, and the unskilled and semi-skilled labourers in my constituency get something like thirty-two and sixpence per week.

For this reason, not only are they denied food, clothing and house accommodation, but even the free gifts of God: sunshine and fresh air, for fresh air and sunlight cannot be got in a big proportion of our tenement dwellings.

That seems to me to be a very definite and clear indication as to where the breeding-ground for some of your tuberculosis is to be found, at least. And I am surprised that the Hon. and gallant gentleman gets up as a politician and attempts to defend a state of things which as a medical man would receive his wholesale condemnation.

We have the definite statement in the report: 'We have continued to carry out a policy of rigorous economy because we must save money.'

SIR F. BANBURY: Hear, hear.

MAXTON: A right Hon. gentleman on the other side said hear, hear to the idea of saving money. It was the Right Hon. Baronet, the Member for the City of London.

SIR F. BANBURY: I am ready to answer anything.

MAXTON: I do not think there is an answer to your remark. Last year the number of children in Scotland who died in their first year rose to eleven thousand, six hundred and sixty-four. That is one thousand, two hundred and sixty-five children *more* than in nineteen twenty-one. One thousand, two hundred and sixty-five children who would have lived in nineteen twenty-one.

The Hon. and gallant gentleman says the withdrawal of milk and food supplies from the mother had no effect that is reflected in the statistics. Does he mean to tell me as a medical man that the withdrawal of milk from a baby gives it a better chance of life?

In the course of his professional career, the Hon. Member for Dumfries must have seen thousands of infants under one year suffering, and he must have seen the parents watching over the little one hovering between life and death.,

I only saw one case and that made a mark on me that I shall never lose. I saw a mother struggling with the last ounce of her energy to save the life of an infant and in saving it she lost her own. I am not interested in the statistics of this. I am interested in the tens of thousands of fathers and mothers tonight who are watching over their babies, wondering whether they are going to live or die. If I can strike the public conscience to see that this is absolutely wrong and unjustifiable in a Christian nation, I should think I had rendered some service to my country.

The circular letter reversing the supply of milk and food was issued on the twelfth of March nineteen twenty-two, when the death rate was at a higher point than it had been for many years, due to an epidemic of measles, influenza and whooping-cough. In the same circular letter, the Scottish Health Board intimated it would no longer approve of the provision of hospital accommodation for children suffering from whooping-cough and measles. At a time when an epidemic was raging, these Hon. Gentlemen on the other side of the House, in the interests of saving money, which the Right Hon. Baronet the Member for the City of London approves of, condemned children to remain in the breeding-ground of infection. In the interests of economy they condemned hundreds of children to death, and I call it *murder*! I call the men who initiated the policy murderers. They have blood on their hands – the blood of infants. It is a fearful thing for any man to have on his soul – a cold, callous, deliberate crime in order to save money.

We are prepared to destroy children in the great interest of dividends. We put children out in the front of the fighting-line –

SIR F. BANBURY: On a point of order –

MAXTON: I will not give way. Not for one moment. You are one of the worst in the whole House!

HON. MEMBERS: Sit down!

MAXTON: I certainly will not sit down!

DEPUTY SPEAKER: The Right Hon. Baronet is raising a point of order.

SIR F. BANBURY: Is it in order for an Hon. Member to call other Hon. Members 'murderers'?

HON. MEMBERS: It's true! He's proved it!

DEPUTY SPEAKER: I do not think it is in order for the Hon. Member to use that term.

MAXTON: If the Hon. Baronet will supply me with a word that describes his action, other than that of 'murderer', I will use it. Failing that, I stick to what I have said.

SIR F. BANBURY: On a point of order –

DEPUTY SPEAKER: **(to MAXTON.)** I have already said that to call any Hon. Member of this House by that name is not in order.

MAXTON: There is only one word that applies, and I applied it to all Members who supported the initiation of this policy, and I applied it particularly to the Right Hon. Baronet, the Member for the City of London –

SIR F. BANBURY: On a point of order –

DEPUTY SPEAKER: I hope the Hon. Gentleman will withdraw the remark as applying to any particular Member of this House.

MAXTON: I can never withdraw. I did it deliberately.

OLD HEN: And do you know what happened? They 'suspended' him – threw him out: no *him*, the child murderer – no – it was: Jimmy Maxton, you are guilty of telling the truth in the House of Commons – OUT. **(MAXTON gets up and walks deliberately out of the House of Commons. Followed later by WHEATLEY.)** And Wheatley got up and he said they were murderers, too, and bugger them: it was John Wheatley – OUT.

So Maxton and Wheatley was planning this big campaign all over England and Wales and Scotland to get themselves support – when canny wee Ramsay stepped in . . .

## A cunning ruse

**J. RAMSAY MacDoNALD peeps out from behind the Speaker's Chair.**

MacDONALD:
> I might have known we'd have trouble sooner or later.
> And one of those wild men would be the instigator.
> We must have good manners, dignity, sweet reason.
> These damn'd Glasgow keelies are guilty of treason –

And now they're proposing to storm through the land
Attacking our democracy, red flag in hand;
Mocking our parliament, rousing the rabble
Frightening the voters and stirring up trouble.

If they lose then we all lose, our party is dead
If they win then I'm done for – they'll chop off my head.

Now nothing in my view could possibly be more sinister
So I've conspired and colluded with the Tory Prime Minister.
Democracy will be served, parliament will win
They're too dangerous to be out, so we'll let them back in.

When they're least expecting it – ssh!

**WILLIE GALLACHER enters as J. RAMSAY MacDONALD goes out.**

GALLACHER: Willie Gallacher here again, folks. By now I'm down in London, too – I tried to get into parliament as a Communist for Dundee, but they wouldnae have me so I'm down here working as a journalist on the Party newspaper. I picked up a highly confidential whisper in the House of Commons they were gonnae lift the suspension, so I dashed round to my friend John Wheatley and told him.

**JOHN WHEATLEY in his hotel room. GALLACHER walks in.**

WHEATLEY: Is that a fact? Now that's a bloody nuisance – I've got a whole campaign organised on the basis of being slung out. How dare they let us in?

GALLACHER: Well, if you'll take my advice, you'll publicly demand to be re-instated.

WHEATLEY: What?

GALLACHER: Your constituents have been unrepresented at Westminster for too long.

WHEATLEY: Aye, about two hundred and fourteen years. What are you driving at?

GALLACHER: Look: go down publicly to Westminster and try to force your way in – just ten minutes before they unexpectedly decide to open the doors to you . . .

WHEATLEY: I begin to cotton on – so that way . . .

GALLACHER: It will look as if they've given in to your demands . . .

WHEATLEY: William, you're wasted on the Communist Party – you should have been a Tory Chancellor of the Exchequer.

GALLACHER: I'm working on it. Do you agree?

WHEATLEY: I'll consult my colleagues.

GALLACHER: **(to audience.)** And that's just what they did. Jimmy Maxton goes up to the front door saying let me in, in the name of the people of Bridgeton – the poor constable says I'm sorry in you cannae go – and all the newspapermen is there enjoying the panto, when, right on cue, out rushes the other lads waving their arms – You've won, lads, you've won – the British Parliament has lifted your suspension – what a Mighty Victory! **(Goes.)**

OLD HEN: Away, Willie Gallacher, you're gey clever, but you're a damn fool.

YOUNG HEN: What? That was a rare idea.

OLD HEN: The day they boys were sucked back into the Westminster whirlpool was a black day for every worker in Scotland – aye, and in England, too. If they'd told that lot of bourgeois bum-lickers to stuff their parliament up their backsides, they might have saved the Labour movement. If they'd gone off to the workers and the ordinary party members and organised a rebellion against MacDonald and his tomfoolery, they would have had all the support they needed. And something might just have emerged to shake the mighty ruling-class off the backs of the working people.

YOUNG HEN: Do you think?

OLD HEN: I'm sure. And the one man who could see clear through the whole crafty set-up, the one man who said he wouldnae even go to the Palace of Westminster, great John MacLean – oh, hell, did he no' go and die a couple of months later. And that, my girl, was the blackest day of all for the Scottish working-class.

## Ramsay in power

OLD HEN: Still, onwards and upwards: in a couple of weeks' time they had another election and Labour did even better. The Twentieth-Century Fox himself, Ramsay MacDonald, did a crafty wee deal with the Liberals, and he was asked to form a Labour government – the hopes were running high in Glasgow, I can tell you. Our own government at last. Jimmy Maxton had a great big victory meeting at Rouken Glen. Me and Charlie had a wee blether wi' him afterwards. He thought parliament was going to change.

**Enter JAMES MAXTON and CHARLIE, OLD HEN and YOUNG HEN have cleared the set.**

MAXTON: You see, Charlie, the situation is not exactly cut and dried: the Tories have got more seats than we have, but the Liberals are going to vote against them – so it's certain we *will* be called on to form a government – it's hell of a tricky.

**YOUNG HEN crosses to them.**

MAXTON: Hello, my dear – Charlie, is this your? . . .

CHARLIE: No, no, a good comrade, just a good comrade. We're just good comrades.

MAXTON: Aye, well, good comrade, have no fear: all your hard work will not be wasted: we won't let you down.

YOUNG HEN: I'm sure you won't, Jimmy.

MAXTON: The big problem is: how to make the wealthy disgorge their wealth. It's gonnae take some doin'.

CHARLIE: Aye, aye.

MAXTON: We may have to do one or two things the bankers and the Stock Exchange won't like very much – and that means trouble. But we know that wi' folks like you behind us, we cannae go wrong. Keep up the struggle – **(to YOUNG HEN)** – and the hard work, eh, Charlie? (Goes. Silence. CHARLIE starts to go, then stops, embarrassed.)**

CHARLIE: **(to YOUNG HEN.)** Can I see you home?

YOUNG HEN: Aye.

**They start to walk off. CHARLIE takes her hand.**

**Enter J. RAMSAY MacDONALD golfing with GENERAL THOMPSON.**

GENERAL THOMPSON: Fore! (Ball flies across stage. GENERAL THOMPSON strides off after it.)**

MacDONALD: My policy paid off – we're in – no thanks to
    Maxton, the lanky-haired bossy mouth,
    And I've come up to think, and play golf, here at Lossiemouth.
    I'm choosing my cabinet, and I'm taking advice
    From my friend General Thompson, who's awfully nice.

GENERAL THOMPSON: Fore! **(He charges back again after his ball.)**

MacDONALD: There are those in the party who think I should be democratic.
Consult *them* – that won't work. As Prime Minister one must
be – to coin a phrase – more pragmatic:
That means I do what I damn well like, consult who I like,
And blame the workers if anything goes wrong.

GENERAL THOMPSON: Fore! **(Crosses yet again after his ball.)**

MacDONALD: Mind you, I can't understand why he insists on
wearing his uniform on the Lossiemouth Golf Course – possibly
so he won't get lost in the rough – and talking of getting lost
in the rough –
Now, I'm the PM and Foreign Office, too
And I'd be everything else, but there'd be too much to do,
I'd have no time for golf or anything.
Good, loyal, right-wingers, in all the key jobs
The problem remains – how to fob off the yobs.
I've had one idea that fits in rather neatly
I'll offer the coal mines to that Bolshevik Wheatley.

**WHEATLEY strides on.**

WHEATLEY: I refuse.

GENERAL THOMPSON: Fore!

**WHEATLEY and J. RAMSAY MacDoNALD crouch as ball flies over. GENERAL THOMPSON goes, taking ball with him. WHEATLEY also goes.**

MacDONALD: What one can't win by cunning, one must win by stealth
I'll offer him trouble – Housing and Health.

WHEATLEY: **(crosses)** I accept. **(He ducks, expecting GENERAL THOMPSON. Nothing.)** It's alright, Ramsay.

MacDONALD: Now I must rush to Aberdeen, avoiding the statue of Wallace –
I've a train to the south, and to Buckingham Palace.

**Enter KING GEORGE V to suitably regal music.**

KING GEORGE V: So we are to call upon a socialist government? Grandmamma would rather jump up on the table and show her knickers.

We suppose we might as well let them play at being Prime Ministers and Home Secretaries, that sort of thing – as far as we can see it won't make any difference to anything serious – our City owns all our money, our industrialists own our industries, our Church owns the minds of our people, and whatever happens, we shall still be king. We have our army, our navy, our air force and our police constables to see to that. **(J. RAMSAY MacDONALD in court dress, bobbing and bowing.)** Ah – J. Ramsay MacDonald – what do you want?

MacDONALD: Sire, I know the country's not going the way your grandmother meant.
But I really would like to have a wee shot at government.
Just a year or a year and a half, eighteen months, something like that.

KING GEORGE V: Yes, so they tell us. But look here, if you're going to pretend you're Prime Minister, you must do us the elementary courtesy of cutting out the silly songs.

MacDONALD: Sire, there is but one song, sire, I desire, sire, to sing –
And that, sire, save your reverence – *God Save The King*.

KING GEORGE V: Yes, we know all that.

MacDONALD: Do you know the second verse, sir, it's all about the Scots . . . ?

KING GEORGE V: Yes, we are the king – now. You, Mr MacDonald, presided at a rally, we think you call it, at Prince Albert's Hall at which our subjects sang not only the *Red Flag*, but also – dreadful to relate – the *Marseillaise*! Today the *Marseillaise*, Mr MacDonald, tomorrow the guillotine.

MacDONALD: I don't know that one, sire. How does it go?

KING GEORGE V: It's F sharp: with a heavy down-beat – ha-ha.

MacDONALD: Sire, I *did* protest, I said it was a disgrace.
But a horrid man from Glasgow told me to shut my face.

KING GEORGE V: Well, don't let it happen again.

MacDONALD: Only by hard persuasion
And clucking like a spinster
Can I stop the *Red Flag* being sung
In the Palace of Westminster.
But I shall stop their yodelling, from their mouths I'll wean it –
Or make quite sure that if they do sing,
They certainly won't mean it.

KING GEORGE V: Good, we can see you are our man. We, of course, are above politics.

MacDONALD: Yes, we are, sir –

KING GEORGE V: No, *we* are. Kindly ensure that the rest of your government is made up of honest, God-fearing, respectable bum-lickers like yourself, or we'll dissolve you.

MacDONALD: Sire, my earnest –

KING GEORGE V: **(shouts)** Get out! We are a busy man!

**J. RAMSAY MacDONALD goes out backwards, bowing. KING GEORGE V yawns.**

MacDONALD My regards to the rest of the family, sire. Sorry to hear about wee George's stammer.

KING GEORGE V: We think the neck's safe in the hands of those fools – We're off to the Tower to play with our jewels . . .

**Goes, humming.**

**Backdrop changes to Glasgow. MULRINE living-room is set.**

## Meanwhile, back in Glasgow

WHEATLEY: **(in spotlight.)** While politicians are manoeuvering, children are starving, mothers weeping, men idle, slums inhabited and wars are being bred. While there is one family starving in Scotland, no Clyde Member will ca' canny at Westminster. The struggle must not be confined to the House of Commons. Labour must mobilize all its forces. The millions who have now voted Labour should, be ready to stand or move as Labour calls. All our eggs must not be found in the parliamentary basket.

**During WHEATLEY's speech, scene changes to HEN's interior. CHARLIE sits in there on his own, looking dejected. OLD HEN calls across to YOUNG HEN, who has been listening to WHEATLEY – and points to CHARLIE.**

OLD HEN: Psst –!

YOUNG HEN: What's up wi' him?

OLD HEN: Away in and find out; maybe he's waiting for you.

YOUNG HEN: Where's my mother?

OLD HEN: Oot.

YOUNG HEN: My faither?

OLD HEN: Oot.

YOUNG HEN: Ma brother?

OLD HEN: Oot, Oot, Oot – the lot of them. What an opportunity . . .

YOUNG HEN: Oh, God aye, you're right – what am I keeping him waiting for? **(She goes into the scene.)** Hello, Charlie – what're you lookin' so glum for? If you can gie me the answer in less than two hours.

CHARLIE: Oh – this an' that.

YOUNG HEN: You feelin' a'right?

CHARLIE: Aye – no' bad.

YOUNG HEN: Are you no' even gonnae look at me?

CHARLIE: **(looks up, smiles)** Ah, you're no' such a bad sight, hen – and you're a bloody good worker – do you no' resent just doin' the dirty work a' the time?

YOUNG HEN: That's what I want to do – I'm no orator – it's worth fighting for, and we fought and won.

CHARLIE: **(goes back to original gloom)** Aye.

YOUNG HEN: Oh, now what have I said? We've got our *own* government, right? And you and me put them there –right? I thought that's what you wanted.

CHARLIE: **(angry)** It's a bloody lum-hat government like a' the rest. Listen to this. **(Reads.)**

'It is a cabinet of old and ageing men; the average age is nearly sixty. It is a cabinet of dullish men with a large contingent of recruits who have spent most of their lives in the Tory or Liberal parties. It is a cabinet largely of rich men and of men who have inherited comfortable fortunes: of capitalists or landlords or brewers.

'So far as Labour is concerned, many of them have never even worked for their living at all, let alone had experience of poverty. And, as for Socialism, not more than five or six of, the whole twenty would call themselves Socialists, and each one of them would give a different, definition of that much-abused term . . . '**(Stops reading.)**

Do you want to hear any more? About Lord Haldane or Lord Parmoor: '. . . the most dreary and most reactionary of all Tory opponents of social reforms . . . ' ?

YOUNG HEN: No. I can guess it.

CHARLIE: Or would you like to hear this quote from Carlyle: 'No party has been so sold since Judas concluded his trade'?

YOUNG HEN: Still, John Wheatley's in there.

CHARLIE: What the hell can he do, with this lot on his back – he needs pushing, no' pulling does John.

YOUNG HEN: Is that what's bothering you?

CHARLIE: No. No' just that. I'm out of work. I've been combed out. Weirs was laying off two hundred – I was number seven. Every red in the shop got thrown out. I get the boot for what? For working to put in a bunch of failed Tories. **(Gets up.)** I'm away to the pub.

YOUNG HEN: No, you are not. Sit down or I'll batter you. Right, that's better. Now – what was it you came to see my father about?

CHARLIE: See your father? Oh – well, no – aye. . . . Er – I didnae come to see your father. Or your mother. Or your brother. I came to see you.

YOUNG HEN: Oh aye! What needs doin'?

CHARLIE: Well – nothin' needs doin', so much. **(Pause.)** I came to tell you. This is gonnae sound hell of a stupid. No.

YOUNG HEN: What?

CHARLIE: Well – I came to tell you that if circumstances had been different, I would have been coming round to say something quite different, but as they are what they are – I'm not.

YOUNG HEN: Not what?

CHARLIE: Going to say something quite different.

YOUNG HEN: Oh. I see.

CHARLIE: And noo I'm goin'.

YOUNG HEN: Wait a minute, I'm still trying to work that out. What *would* you have said if whatever had been whatever?

CHARLIE: No – I'm no' tellin' you that.

YOUNG HEN: For Christ's sake –

CHARLIE: Cheerio. **(Goes.)**

**She runs after him and catches him up.**

YOUNG HEN: Charlie . . . were you meanin' – anything personal?

CHARLIE: Och, hell – I luv ye. But I'm broke.

YOUNG HEN: Oh, here, that's wonderful . . .

CHARLIE: Wonderful?

YOUNG HEN: It's really romantic.

CHARLIE: Do you think so? But be a bit practical.

YOUNG HEN: Right. I'll be practical. Will you marry me?

CHARLIE: **(laughs)** You'll have to ask my father . . .

YOUNG HEN: Come on, let's go down and look at the river. I'm told it's the thing to do – and there's a full moon as well.

**They go and look at the river, with ripple-lighting effect used without too much subtlety over the whole set. Music in. A romantic song of the period, such as *The Moon Belongs to Everyone*, is sung by a smooth SINGER in a tuxedo. An artificial full moon on a stick bobs up and down romantically behind the Glasgow tenement backdrop. The essence of the song remains: the trappings – tuxedo, SINGER's manner, piano style, lighting, moon effect, are sent up. On last note of song, lights go out.**

**The OLD HEN, who should be playing the piano, mischievously accompanying her own young romance, gets up as the lights come up again.**

OLD HEN: **(to audience.)** And that was how I got my man, Charlie Sullivan. **(Enter YOUNG HEN.)**

YOUNG HEN: Here, Granny – that was lovely.

OLD HEN: And did I no' choose the right moment? Not only was he out of work, he was on the black-list – Weirs had given his name to every engineering employer in the West of Scotland: troublemaker – no thank you, get out. And to make matters worse, that wonderful Labour government we put in did nothing – for Charlie, for me, for naebody.

The only one who got anywhere was Wheatley – he was *determined* to do something about decent houses for folks to live in, and he got a – start made on that, but even he was no' so sure.

**JOHN WHEATLEY comes on and stands on one side of them.**

WHEATLEY: At the present moment workers' representatives are powerless in the House of Commons, and I personally do not treat it very seriously, but regard it as a second or third-rate debating society. The country is being driven either to national ruin or bloody revolution.

OLD HEN: And as for Jimmy Maxton . . .

**JAMES MAXTON comes on the other side, angry.**

MAXTON: Geordie Buchanan has put up his Home Rule for Scotland Bill. By Christ I hope it gets through. I want to go to Euston, St Pancras or Kings Cross, and book a single ticket for Glasgow. I, for one, would be delighted never to go back to London again. Well – I might go down for the international, or to hear the Orpheus choir, or something worth-while – but never for the sake of legislating for the British Empire.

I could ask no greater job in life than to make English-ridden, capitalist-ridden, landowner-ridden Scotland into the Scottish Socialist Commonwealth – and in doing that, I'd be doing a great service to the people of England, Wales and the world. **(He and WHEATLEY go.)**

YOUNG HEN: Here – what happened to that Home Rule Bill?

OLD HEN: Nothin'. Before they could even castrate it, they were out, the lot of them – on the burroo, like Charlie. Canny wee Ramsay called another election, but he wasnae as canny as the Tories. The Tories got back in. That put the kibosh on it. Enter Winston Churchill and his cronies all set to smash the workers right back into the ground – six feet under if possible.

They were bitter months, girl, and the unemployment in Glasgow was gettin' worse – Charlie gave up hope of gettin' a job ever again. But still, we were to be married. May

QUEEN MARGARET UNIVERSITY LRC

nineteen twenty-five. It would have been my Golden Weddin'
this year. **(Pauses to think.)** What was I tellin' ye? Aye – we
was to be married, an' my mother was all for us stayin' with
her – but there was this awfie carry on about sleeping
arrangements . . .

## Sleeping arrangements

**YOUNG HEN goes into scene as MOTHER is talking to
CHARLIE. GEORGE sits silently.**

MOTHER: Now, Charlie, you've no choice but to stay – and I
don't object in the slightest. **(GEORGE stirs.)** Oh, come on
now, George, will you stop bloody arguing? Look, before wee
Agnes died, you know fine it was Henrietta and Agnes in
there, and me and Freddie through there, and you on the
floor here. **(GEORGE looks away.)** God grant me patience,
you're aye goin' on at me. Alright, so when wee Agnes died
me and your father moved in there, Henrietta on the floor
here and you got the room to youself. Bloody lucky you were
too. I know, you've no need to keep goin' on at me – but
surely to Christ you can see that the newlyweds must have
the room floor to theirsel's, and you must come in here – it's
no gonnae kill you. **(GEORGE sniffs.)** Shut up! I *know* Freddie
snores – fit to shake the lums off the roof – I *know* – but if *I*
can put up wi' it and she can put up wi' it, so can *you*.
**(GEORGE scratches his nose.)** . . . George, if you're worried
about that, Friday nights you can stay out – God, he's got an
answer for everything, so he has.

**GEORGE gets up and goes out.**

MOTHER: **(Shocked)** Where's he off? – Ach, pay no heed to him.
He'll come back. You'll both stay wi' us, right? Henrietta's
working – she can gie me money for the two of you. . . . Now

you'll take some potted heid, right, Charlie. Do you know somethin', girl – I've a soft spot for Charlie – you'll need to keep an eye on him. **(She goes off to the kitchen.)**

CHARLIE: I'm sorry, love. I'm – humiliated.

YOUNG HEN: You've nothin' to be sorry for, Charlie. I'm sorry for you – no, I'm not sorry. I'm bloody *angry*. And as for that brother of mine – ach, I suppose it was the war.

CHARLIE: I went through the war, too, hen, I had no bloody option.

YOUNG HEN: Do you want to tell me about it?

CHARLIE: No. It's just – it wasnae worth it . . .

**As YOUNG HEN and CHARLIE sit together, uncomfortably, a quiet song comes in.**

SINGER: *You catch my eye and then you look away –*
*That secret world you lived in yesterday*
*Has locked up your heart in some cold prison cell,*
*Locked me out in the night from your sad private hell –*
*But a secret despair never dies – won't you tell –*
*Have you locked up your heart forever?*

*You went to war but why you could not say –*
*Maybe strangers but they were brothers you killed that fine day:*
*You went out with a gun to shoot men with no name,*
*Your bayonet tore open bodies with shame*
*You stifled your cries and your tears and your blame –*
*And you locked up your heart forever –*

*Forget your yesterday*
*Forget your secret sorrow,*
*We've love to share today*
*A new world to build tomorrow:*

*And when these wars are of the past*
*We'll build a peace that's made to last*
*In the world we'll build – tomorrow . . .*

**The song, or the thoughts that the song has expressed for them both, has drawn them closer together.**

**Enter GEORGE with suitcase. They watch him as he goes and picks up his bag of tools and dumps them beside the suitcase in the middle of the floor. He pulls his jumping jack out from under the cupboard and puts it in his pocket. MOTHER comes in and watches.**

MOTHER: George, what you doin'?

**GEORGE indicates leaving.**

MOTHER: What do you mean, – goin'? – Where to?

**GEORGE, same gesture.**

MOTHER: Away ta-ta?

FATHER: **(enters)** What's goin' on here – George, will you no' speak, man?

**Pause.**

GEORGE: Aye, I will. The room's gonnae be vacant – if her an him's wantin' to get married, they can sleep in there – it's free – I'm for the aff.

YOUNG HEN: George, you don't have to just because . . .

GEORGE: I've got a room in a boarding house. Five shillins a week includin' washin'. I'm no' stayin' here tae rot – I'm settin' up in business on my own. I've got a wee workshop, and I'll have two carpenters startin' for me Monday morning: do you think I don't mean it?

MOTHER: Look, son, you sit down a wee minute, you'll no' be feeling just too good, eh?

GEORGE: I've never felt better.

**Pause.**

FATHER: You need money for that kind of thing, George.

GEORGE: See that? My bank book. I've been puttin' it away since nineteen nineteen – now I've got what I needed – two hundred pounds – that's capital. I've been workin' for some other man long enough. I've been watchin'. I know how it's done. Now there's gonnae be fellas workin' for me.

FATHER: What are they gonnae do – I mean, what *line*?

GEORGE: Coffins, doors, wee toys, see . . . **(Shows jumping jack.)**

CHARLIE: George – can you no' see?

GEORGE: Aye, I can see – I can see what you and your bloody politics and unions and agitatin's done for us – I can see – I watched and I waited – sure enough – nothin'. You and your schemin's no' gonnae do anything for me till I'm in the ground – so I'm doin' somethin' for mysel' – and I'm gonnae make it – I'm gonnae have a workshop the size of this street, with a yard full of mahogany and ash and walnut and a house, my own house, wi' an inside lavvy, and a front bloody garden, and domestic servants, and a car, with a chauffeur and curtains on the windows and a speakin' tube, and I'm gonnae have a bank account, wi' my money in it – and naebody's gonnae stop me. Because I've planned it. **(GEORGE opens suitcase,** takes out overcoat and bowler.) See: that's mine. That's something, that. **(To CHARLIE and YOUNG HEN.)** What you two's dreamin' of is *nothing* – right. I'm gonnae put this on tae walk down the street – and I'm no' coming back.

MOTHER: You're no' coming back?

GEORGE: I'll send word where you can find me. I'll send you my card.

FATHER: But, son – what are you doin' this for?

GEORGE: I'm fed up bein' a working-class fool. **(Puts on bowler, goes.)**

MOTHER: **(a touch of pride.)** I'm gonnae watch him walk down the street. **(She goes after him.)**

FATHER: For Chris' sake! **(Goes into the other room.)**

YOUNG HEN: Does he mean a' that?

CHARLIE: Aye.

YOUNG HEN: What are we gonnae do?

CHARLIE: Get married. Sleep in the kitchen. We've no money and no prospects – but we've got somethin', hen – something . . . poor George,

OLD HEN: An' a' the bairns in the street stopped their play to watch him go.

**SINGER marches into middle of room. Phrase on piano.**

SINGER: **(sings)** *My maw's a millionaire.*

YOUNG HEN/CHARLIE: **(sing)** *Would you believe it?*

SINGER: **(sings)** *Blue eyes, and curly hair,*
   *Walking down Buchanan Street,*
   *Wi' her big banana feet,*
   *Ma maw's a millionaire.*

**The whole COMPANY comes on and sings it again, then sing individually or together:**

SINGER: *Old Mother Riley at the pawnshop door*
   *A baby in her arms and a bundle on the floor,*
   *She asked for ten bob, and she only got four,*
   *She nearly took the hinges off the old man's door –*

ALL: *Our wee school's the best wee school*
   *The best wee school in Glesa*
   *The only thing that's wrong wi' it's*
   *The baldy wee headmaster.*

   *He goes to the pub on a Saturday night*
   *He goes to the church on Sunday*
   *He prays to the Lord to gie him strength*
   *Tae belt the weans on Monday.*

SINGER: *The Big Ship was leaving Bombay –*
   *Today –*
   *Bound for the Isle of Man*
   *So they say –*
   *Along came Henrietta with tears in her eyes,*
   *Along came Charlie with two big black eyes,*
   *Saying:*

CHARLIE: *Darling oh Darling be mine, be mine,*
   *I'll send you a sweet Valentine:*

SINGER: *He turned round to kiss her,*
   *She ducked and he missed her –*

ALL: *The Big Ship was leaving Bombay – Today.*

GEORGE: *If you see a big fat wumman*
*Staunin' on the corner bummin'*
**(Stamp.)** *That's ma mammy.*
*If you see a wee thin fella*
*Like a rolled-up umbrella*
**(Stamp.)** *That's ma daddy.*

YOUNG HEN: *When oor da' gets another job*
*Each week he'll earn fifty bob.*
*We'll a' be like folk in Bearsden*
*Wi' carpet flairs an' lavvies ben.*
*In and oot the Parish*
*In and oot the Parish*

*In and oot the Parish*

*God bless the Unemployed.*
*Like Mary Rae who jeers us all*
*We'll wear a coat an' no' a shawl*
*The plates o' peas we'll leave alone*
*For we'll hae links an' tattie scones.*

*In and oot the Parish, etc.*

*Oor maw will hae a stuck-up nose*
*For we will stay in a wally close*
*We'll be sae rich an' no' the same*
*Well even ken the factor's name.*

*In and oot the Parish, etc.*

FATHER: *There is a happy land down Duke Street Jail*
*Where a' the prisoners stand, tied to a nail*
*Ham and eggs they never see*
*Dirty water for their tea*
*That's the place for you and me*
*God Save the Queen.*

OLD HEN: *Oh ye cannae shove yer grannie off a bus.*

ALL: *Quite right, too.*

OLD HEN: *No ye cannae shove yer grannie off a bus*
  *Oh ye cannae shove yer grannie –*

YOUNG HEN: *For she's yer mammy's mammy –*

OLD HEN: *No ye cannae shove yer grannie off a bus.*

**ALL sing this again as one of the COMPANY says that it's interval time, and there's a bar, so I will if you will, so will I . . .**

ALL: *Singing I will if you will so will I*
  *Singing I will if you will so will I*
  *Singing I will if you will*
  *I will if you will,*
  *I will if you will, so will I.*

# Act 2

**As Lights go down, CHARLIE and FATHER come on to room set and pace anxiously up and down.**

**OLD HEN comes on shouting for HENRIETTA, who is amongst the audience.**

OLD HEN: Have you seen that girl? She's never here when I want her. Henrietta, where the hell are you? Are you down there selling shares in Scotland's oil?

YOUNG HEN: Gie's a break.

OLD HEN: I'm wantin' you.

YOUNG HEN: I'm busy.

OLD HEN: It's the young men you're after, is it? Put that man down, he's old enough to be your grandfather.

YOUNG HEN: I'm just sortin' out these Liberals **(in the circle/at the bar/over here, etc.)**

OLD HEN: Liberals? In here? God, if there's one thing worse than a Tory it's a Liberal — where are they — I'll sort them out mysel'.

YOUNG HEN: No, Gran. I've given them a good speakin'-to, they'll no' cause any bother. **(Comes up on to stage.)**

OLD HEN: Right — now I've a wee bit more to tell you before I'm done. See these two here?

YOUNG HEN: What's up wi' them?

OLD HEN: Nineteen twenty-six! And the house of Mulrine is in a state of high nervous tension! . . . Was it because of the unemployment?

CHARLIE/FATHER: **(together)** No.

OLD HEN: Was it because there was a Tory government intent on smashing the workers?

CHARLIE/FATHER: **(together)** No.

OLD HEN: Was it because capitalism was entering an almighty crisis, a deep depression, a black despair?

CHARLIE/FATHER: **(together)** No.

YOUNG HEN: What was it then?

OLD HEN: Sssh!

**A baby's cry, from off. Music in, CHARLIE jumps up in the air with delight, and FATHER shakes his hand. CHARLIE comes down to sing: *You Can Come and See the Baby*, a Will Fyfe number – or another suitable old song to celebrate the birth of a baby – father's version. The FAMILY join in the last chorus. At the end, CHARLIE is led in by MOTHER, to see the baby.**

OLD HEN: Aye. Only thing was – it was a girl. Joan – your mother.

YOUNG HEN: Oh, God – here, my mother was born in that house? Wi' her father out of work? You're kiddin' me on . . .

OLD HEN: Do you think I'm likely to forget?

YOUNG HEN: And she's the one that's tellin' me how I ought to meet some nice young men, so why don't I join the Young Conservatives?

OLD HEN: Aye, well, she's come up in the world, eh – got herself a high-rise flat in Garngad –

YOUNG HEN: Oh no, we don't call it that any more – it's known as Royston Hill now we've moved in . . . the man up the stair's daein' eight years for armed robbery and the fella down the stair's daein' life for sawin' heads off wi' a hacksaw – but to hear my mother you'd think it was some sort of upper-class monastery.

OLD HEN: She's been a pain in the backside ever since she went scrubbin' floors in Newton Mearns . . .

YOUNG HEN: Did you know Mrs Tomlinson drove her through to Edinburgh, and the pair of them stood wavin' Union Jacks at Margaret Thatcher?

OLD HEN: God – what a stimulatin' experience – ach, the working-class has aye had problems like Joan: the problem is most of them end up on the General Council of the TUC. And the year she was born was the year that lot came out in their true colours . . . nineteen twenty-six. I was a shop steward at the time, and when I got back to the sweatshop after your mother was born, I could see the way things were going: the system was in trouble, trade was no' boomin', even the coal owners were losin' money – so *we* were under attack. The only thing between them and us was the unions. Somebody had to stand up and say NO. As usual it was the miners – right out in front, ready to take a batterin'.

## The implacable foe

OLD HEN: **(continues.)** But they were nae just havin' a go at the miners. Big Chief Baldwin spilt the beans, when some of the miners went to see him . . .

**BALDWIN and MINER come on, try to pass each other, do, then recognise each other.**

BALDWIN: Ah, you're a coal-miner.

MINER: Ah, you're a Prime Minister.

BALDWIN: Yes. Now then, industry is confronted with a difficult situation. You chaps will just have to jolly well make your contribution.

MINER: Do you mean get oor wages cut?

BALDWIN: Yes, I do. All the workers in this country have got to face a reduction in wages.

MINER: A reduction in wages? What do you mean?

BALDWIN: I mean – I shall say it again, and every Prime Minister including your own Bolshevik Harold Wilson will say it after me.

MINER: You can say that again.

BALDWIN: I shall say it again and every Prime. Minister including your own Bolshevik Harold Wilson will say it after me. I mean all the workers in this country have got to take reductions in wages to help put British industry on its feet.

MINER: Is that a fact? Well, I say to you and every British miner will say it after me – get knotted!

BALDWIN: You'd better not say that again.

MINER: Get knotted. Twice.

**They go off.**

OLD HEN: Aye, capitalism was buggered; just like it is now. And the only way they could make it work was to take money out of the pockets of the workers. Just like it is now. The only consolation then was that it was a Tory government.

YOUNG HEN: Just like it is now.

OLD HEN: So you can tell a Tory when you see one?

YOUNG HEN: Aye –

OLD HEN: Except when it's in a kilt –

YOUNG HEN: Will you get on with the story, and stop provokin' me? She's a bigot, so she is.

OLD HEN: Every trade unionist in the country rallied to defend the miners, right? Not a minute on the day, not a penny off the pay – right? Or the whole country's coming out – right?, Ya bas. The Tories beat a crafty retreat: OK – the subsidy will go on to the first of May nineteen twenty-six. They were giving themselves time to prepare for a fight. And they intended to win, so by the first of May 1926 they were ready. But were we?

**Enter J. RAMSAY MacDONALD.**

MacDONALD: As far as we can see we shall go on. I don't like General Strikes. I haven't changed my opinion. I have said so in the House of Commons. I don't like it; honestly: I don't like it; but, honestly, what can be done?

By the way, I'm the leader of the Labour Party. Honestly.

MRS BEATRICE WEBB: Poor Ramsay! Dear Diary – 'We personally are against the use of the General Strike in order to force the government to submit to the men's demands. If it were to succeed it would mean a militant minority were starving the majority into submission – and that would be the end of democracy.'

By the way, my husband agrees with me – and he's chairman of the Labour Party. Come on, Ramsay – **(produces handkerchief)** – big blow – **(He blows. They go.)**

OLD HEN: The diddy men . . . Aye, but it wasnae just the politicians. The miners' leaders stood firm as a rock, but they had to put the matter in the hands of the General Council of the British TUC.

**Enter, to music, some of the General Council of the TUC, 1926.**

TUC: **(sing)** *We're the British TUC, TUC, TUC.*
*We're the British TUC, let's do a deal –*
*We don't want a revolution*
*To change the constitution*
*That's not our cuppa tea you see.*

*– Let's do a deal –*

*The Tories aren't waiting*
*While we're cogitating*
*Volunteers they are massing*
*While we sit here gassing*
*They've organisations*
*To run railway stations*
*They've student tram-drivers*
*With monocles and fivers*
*They've black-leg coal miners*
*Protest and they'll fine us –*

*Our members have pleaded*
*That we do what's needed.*

*So we formed a Committee*
*But Oh what a pity.*

*Were the British TUC*
*We've done sod all.*

WALTER CITRINE: Comrades and friends – I don't like saying that, but I've got to –my name is Walter Citrine. I'm not a Lord yet, but I bloody soon will be – meantime I'm the General Secretary of this outfit. The union members are trying to tell us what to do – they want a General Strike. But *I* say what goes, that's what I'm paid for. Well negotiate a settlement – on behalf of the miners – won't we, lads?

OTHERS: Aye, Walter, aye, Walter, aye aye aye.

CITRINE: Not that I'm not democratic: oh no – TUC does not stand for Trampled Under Citrine, as some wit remarked. God rest his soul. No – it means Tolerance – under Citrine. So they can all shut their cake-holes, I don't fancy General Strikes, too much paper work. Let's go and do a deal with Baldwin while the miners aren't looking. I like going to Number Ten Downing Street, you get your picture in the paper – come on, lads . . .

BALDWIN: **(in pyjamas and top hat)** Negotiations are broken off. And I've gone to bed. Go away. **(Produces teddy-bear.)** Come on, Teddy. **(Goes.)**

CITRINE: Oh dear – now were for it. . . .

ALL: **(sing)** *They've soldiers, and sailors*
*Policemen and gaolers*
*They'll surely defeat us –*
*Then Churchill will eat us . . .*
*AArgh! - for breakfast, on toast.*
*They'll come for you and me, you see –*
*Let's do a deal.*

**They go off in terror.**

OLD HEN: That Executive grovelled, it cringed, it begged Baldwin to think of a way to stop them calling a General Strike. That was when Baldwin and Churchill and Lord Birkenhead and the other generalissimos of the ruling class knew they were on a winner. Their side was organised, ours was unprepared, feart, and weak at the top. Go ahead – says Baldwin – call your strike – and we'll smash you.

**Enter CHARLIE to house, with blood pouring from his head.**

MOTHER: **(from offstage)** Is that you, Freddie? **(Comes on.)** Charlie! What in the name of . . . Come here till I see. **(FATHER comes in.)** Freddie, will you get a cloth or somethin'?

CHARLIE: Ach, I'm alright . . .

FATHER: What happened to you?

CHARLIE: Nothin' – we heard there was blackleg tram-drivers in Dalmarnock tram depot – about four or five hundred miners from Newton and Cambuslang came in tae help us picket the place, that's all . . .

MOTHER: So who walloped you?

CHARLIE: There was more bloody polis than I've ever seen in the whole of my life. They came down on us like a pack of wolves – look at that . . . **(Shows jacket ripped right up the back.)**

FATHER: Never mind that – what about that? **(Points to his head.)**

CHARLIE: I'm no' feelin' just so steady on my pins . . .

MOTHER: Oh Christ, where's the lassie?

CHARLIE: She's away to Carlton Place, to give the word to the Trades Council – on a bicycle.

MOTHER: On a bicycle – but she cannae ride one –

CHARLIE: She's just found out.

MOTHER: Here, I'll get you somethin' to wash yoursel'. **(Goes.)**

CHARLIE: D'you hear about they students in Edinburgh? Tried to drive a train – Christ knows how but they smashed it up in a tunnel – three people got killed.

FATHER: Aye – it's a terrible thing.

**MOTHER comes back with rag**.

MOTHER: Here, I'm that worried about that lassie.

CHARLIE: Och, she'll be alright – oh Christ! That bike.

MOTHER: What?

CHARLIE: Well, it's just – I told her how tae go it, but I didnae tell her how to stop . . .

OLD HEN: **(laughing)** But I found out all by myself – when I got tae Jamaica Bridge there was this wee student in plus-fours tryin' to direct the traffic – he'd volunteered so the real polis could go and crack a few skulls – I thought to mysel' right, you wee bastard – and I drove straight at him, yellin' help, help, I cannae stop, I cannae stop! and the gallant wee manny haulds out his hand, and I grabs it – well. . . . **(Sings)** *He flew through the air with the greatest of ease* – and I fell off; another casualty in the class war.

And all over England and Wales and Scotland, the strike got bigger and better organised, and stronger – you see, we were sure we were goin' to win. We had tae – we knew what wis waitin' for us if we lost . . .

**Lights change. TWO MEMBERS of COMPANY come on to read, as themselves, from newspapers, etc., of the time. (These readings can vary to suit locality of performance.)**

1st READER: The main unions called out in support of the miners were the railwaymen, the transport workers, the builders, the iron and steel workers. After one week of the strike, the printers, engineers and shipyard workers came out. In all cases, the strikes were almost one hundred per cent solid.

2nd READER: *British Gazette*, the official organ of the government during the strike. 'All ranks of the Armed Forces of the Crown are hereby notified that any action which they may find it necessary to take in an honest endeavour to aid the

Civil Power will receive both now and afterwards the full support of His Majesty's Government.'

1st READER: Cardinal Bourne: 'There is no moral justification for a General Strike. It is therefore a sin against the obedience which we owe to God. All are bound to uphold and assist the Government which is the lawfully constituted authority of the country and represents, therefore, the authority of God himself.'

2nd READER: Lord Reith, General Manager of the BBC, to Mr Baldwin: 'Assuming that the BBC is for the people, and that the government is for the people, it follows that the BBC must be for the government.'

1st READER: American observer at London docks: 'I saw enough artillery to kill every living thing in every street in the neighbourhood.'

2nd READER: Sir John Simon, former Liberal Home Secretary: 'Every trade union leader is liable in damages to the uttermost farthing of his personal possessions.'

1st READER: The Hon. Mrs Beaumont undertook stable duties at Paddington Station.

2nd READER: Unemployed car salesman: 'I'd always been mad on model railways, and of course, my dream was to drive a train. I was really in my element.'

1st READER: A train which left Manchester on Tuesday at nine-thirty a.m. is reported to have arrived in London at ten-fifteen a.m. Friday.

2nd READER: Undergraduate: 'We set out from Oxford early in the evening in a vintage Bentley and drove at great speed through the lovely English countryside. At Doncaster our driver stood us dinner and a bottle of champagne. From Doncaster onwards, groups of strikers tried to interrupt our progress by occasionally throwing stones and trying to puncture our tyres. However, our driver remained unperturbed and merely accelerated when he saw a hostile crowd – at times we reached eighty miles an hour. On the following day I started work on Glasgow docks.'

**The THREE ACTORS in the scene have been listening. They now break in.**

3rd READER: **(Charlie)** Peter Kerrigan, Glasgow Trades Council, Strike Co-ordinating Committee: (And you'll no' find this in the *British Gazette*.) 'The majority of strike-breakers in Glasgow were recruited from the students. They tried to move lorries from the docks and man trams, mainly in the centre. But they couldn't move half a mile without being smashed up and the lorries from the docks had to have a military escort. It was a long time before what the students did was forgotten.'

4th READER: **(Father)** R. E. Scoular, STUC: 'In and out of the city not a vehicle could move without our sanction. We would have commercial travellers ringing us up highly indignant at being waylaid by gangs of miners. I had an anxious phone-call from one of the pickets – 'What shall we do, the field's full?' 'What field?' 'We're stopping the cars on the road and turning them into a feld.' 'Well, find another field.'

3rd READER: **(Charlie)** Glasgow: eleventh of May nineteen twenty-six. One hundred persons were sentenced to three months imprisonment, twenty-five for longer. Fourteen were from Maryhill, accused of taking part in a disturbance: a procession of young men through the streets, headed by a man playing a melodeon, shouting 'To Hell with the Government' – and other remarks.

4th READER: **(Father)** Will Blyton, Durham miner: 'The Dean of

Durham made a speech saying that the miners were never satisfied. We marched in with banners saying 'To Hell With Bishops, We Want a Living Wage'. The women were so infuriated they pushed him in the river. That night he preached a sermon on the text: Father, forgive them for they know not what they do.'

5th READER: **(Young Hen)** Megan Morgan, South Wales: 'It was beautiful weather that summer, what we call strike weather. It never seemed to rain. Some nights there would be dancing in the streets half the night. The jazz bands would walk from the Rhondda half-starved as they were. We dammed up the river, made a pool and there was bathing by moonlight. Everything was organised: the soup-kitchen, even the boat-repairing was done co-operatively.

3rd READER: **(Charlie)** Dutch, German and Czech miners all solid in support of the British miners. The Canadian, American, French, German, All-India and Russian TUCs sent donations. All accepted – except the Russian, which was sent back.

**The three in the scene return to their set.**

1st READER: Twelfth of May: Deeside – no sign of weakening.

2nd READER: Twelfth of May: Kilmarnock –not the slightest sign of weakening.

1st READER: Twelfth of May: Denny and Dunipace – no weakening.

2nd READER: Twelfth of May: Bo'ness – no weakening.

1st READER: Twelfth of May: Bermondsey, London – no sign of weakening whatever.

2nd READER: Twelfth of May: Birkenhead – no weakening, stoppage extending.

1st READER: Twelfth of May: Wolverhampton – no weakening.

2nd READER: Twelfth of May: Wakefield – no sign of weakening.

1st READER: Twelfth of May: Glasgow . . .

**Back into house. ALL there, as before. YOUNG HEN runs in with a newspaper.**

YOUNG HEN: Here, look at that.

CHARLIE: What are you doin' readin' that scab's daily for?

YOUNG HEN: Read it . . .

CHARLIE: What does it say?

YOUNG HEN: It says the strike's called off. The General Council of the TUC has given in – unconditional surrender.

CHARLIE: Ach away –

YOUNG HEN: It's been announced on the wireless, Charlie – it's *true* – and the bosses are ecstatic – listen . . .

'Not since Armistice Day has the city heard any news which has given, greater satisfaction.' Then inside – 'No union member formerly employed on the Glasgow Herald need apply for re-instatement.'

CHARLIE: So they've begun already . . .

FATHER: For what have they stopped it?

CHARLIE: **(forcefully, angrily)** I don't know.

MOTHER: Still an' all, thank God it's all over.

CHARLIE: You'll no' be thanking God in a month or two, Nora, were all gonnae suffer – we've fought and we've lost – now we're gonnae pay the price. As if we're not paying enough

73

already – the whole working class is gonnae suffer for this for years to come.

**They go off, leaving OLD HEN. YOUNG HEN joins her, and listens, in a quiet, intimate grouping that draws them together.**

## Bone soup

OLD HEN: Aye, and so we did. Soon Charlie wasnae the only one on the parish – there was thousands and thousands queueing for their dole-money – if they were lucky enough to get any. We got another Labour government alright – aye, Ramsay MacDonald rode again – we put him in to increase the benefit – do you know what he did? He cut it. When he came in, one man in ten was unemployed – in two years, one man in five. Do you know what we had to dae? Ah've seen my ain mother traipse on her two feet frae Bridgeton to Skinners in Sauchiehall Street, wi' a pillow-slip tae fill wi' broken loaves that naebody wanted – and, if she was lucky, squashed meringues. The next day she'd be up to the Bermaline for two pennorth of broken biscuits. First Charlie lost his job, then my father, then my mother – I was still going on fine, nineteen shillings a week frae the sweatshop, stitching up ball-gowns and pin-stripe suits. Made me sick to think of people dressin' up like that wi' other people starvin' near to death in the same city – still, it was keepin' me in work: till then what happened? Just what I needed maist in the world – twins.

YOUNG HEN: You mean my Uncle Freddie in Vancouver?

OLD HEN: Aye, and your Uncle Charlie that was washed away in the floods in Darwin, Australia. Here, did he no' send you a boomerang?

YOUNG HEN: Aye. It didnae work.

OLD HEN: I fed them till they were five months; I was like a rake. I heard you got one and sixpence a week extra frae the parish if you were feeding a wain . . . the bastard asked me if I could prove it – I felt like whippin' one out and gie'n him a squirt in the eye. Still, we got by. Mince and tatties on a Thursday and there was aye bone-soup – if you could get a bone that is. It was hard to get a bone . . . see Jessie Nolan, her they've stuck in the Eventide Home – well she had this great big knee-bone: here, says I – what kind of a beast did you get that off of, an elephant out of the zoo? Don't let on, says she. Here, I says, gie's a lend of it after you've finished with it. Three pots of soup came out of that bone – it went from her pot tae mine, and then tae May Armstrong up the stair – and that's God's truth.

Ach, the thirties was nae time to be trying to get by, in Glasgow or anywhere else – they *had* to start another war, to get the men some work. And our great parliamentary heroes? What did they do? Most of the Great Reds of the Clyde slid into the Labour Party, in the hope of turnin' into Prime Ministers. Not Jimmy Maxton, no – he became a sad, solitary voice, crying in the wilderness. Nor Wheatley. He died. Still a Pape, but still fightin'. And the TUC? Spineless. And then, to cap it all, doesnae Charlie decide he's going off to Spain to do battle with the Fascists? Oh aye – it was the right courageous thing to dae. But was there no' enough to fight here? I telt him – if anyone's gonnae get shot, it'll be you – but no – he knew. Well, I was proved right by a Fascist bullet, wallop, right between the eyes – he was aye pig-headed. Leaving me wi' three wains to bring up – if I could have got a haud of him, I'd have kicked his heed in.

Poor Charlie; we need a few more like him today.

**OLD HEN is by now very upset about Charlie. YOUNG HEN gently leads her off. Song, to tune *Jamies Foyers*, the first verse of Ewan MacColl's song:**

SINGER: *He's gone frae the shipyard that stands on the Clyde*
*His hammer is silent, his tools laid aside;*
*To the wide Ebro River, young Foyers has gone*
*To fecht by the side of the people of Spain.*

**She turns and watches GEORGE come on, then goes.**

## Let's go with Labour

**GEORGE comes into kitchen, looks around, sniffs, mutters. He looks prosperous and bigger.**

GEORGE: Nineteen fifty-one. Well, this is one part of Britain that's not havin' a festival. Pig-sty. To think that in nineteen fifty-one they old folks is still living like pigs. **(To audience.)** I was brought up in this house. Thank Christ we're livin' in a democracy where a fella like me can get out of slums like this. Take me for example. Brother Charlie got a bullet in Spain. I've got a villa. And I come frae *this*. That's democracy.

The last time you clapped your eyes on me, I was settin' up in wood – wee toys, coffins, doors., Well you can keep your wee toys and coffins – they're for kids and corpses, neither of which is particularly big spenders. Doors, that's what held the key. Doors go intae buildings, right – so do door-frames, window-frames, roof-beams, floorboards, flights of stairs and fitted cupboards – the buildin' industry: the only industry apart frae armaments that was booming in the nineteen thirties. I began to get wee contracts for Corporation housing schemes; Knightswood, Carntyre – then I met a bent quantity surveyor on holiday in Largs. We began to see eye to eye, and my contracts expanded. Now I'm married to his daughter, Priscilla – I think that's her name – and I'm daein' very well thank you. Durin' the war I diversified; into Nissen huts, air-raid shelters and officers' messes: important war-work. And thanks to your wee boy, Adolf Hitler, I made a packet. Pre-fabs. Rebuildin'.

After the war, we got ourselves this Labour government – wi' big plans. I began to see the positive aspects of John Wheatley's housing schemes – if you know what I mean? The Glasgow Corporation, seemed set on spending millions of pounds on buildings. I felt, at this point, I needed some political representation myself – so I joined the Labour Party – well, I'm a working-class boy – and got myself elected a councillor. And, now, due to my specialist know-how, I'm on the Building Committee – you might think – in fact you probably certainly do think – I'd have a conflict of interests there – me bein' a contractor to the Corporation an' that, but believe me, there was no conflict – my interests went hand in hand together. But the Moving Finger writes, and having wrote moves on. Now we're into the golden days: Easterhouse, Castlemilk, Drumchapel, Pollock – I'm employin' six hundred men, I cannae go wrong. And now we've started makin' plans for the big one. Enough of mucking around in the suburbs – the whole of the city awaits.

The future lies glowing ahead like a Christmas puddin'. First, a few bob on the side renovatin' the old tenements – that's Phase One. Phase Two, you sell them to Glasgow Corporation. Phase Three, Glasgow Corporation pays you to knock them all down, and Phase Four, and this is where the real profits, or should I say social benefits, come in – you pay me to rebuild the whole shooting-match. Share this vision with me now – mile upon mile of motorway threadin' its way through the elegant, tree-dotted landscapes of Anderston, Partick and Govan, where a contented population dwells in tall, slender towers, shopping effortlessly in spacious shopping centres with purpose-built access roads – and all this due, false modesty be damned, to yours truly, Baillie George Mulrine placing contracts with Mulrine (Motorways)

Ltd; Mulrivert (Vertical Dwelling Units) Ltd; Mulriscape (Environmental Sculptors) Ltd; Mulristorey Car Parks; and Mulresco (Easyspend Trading Arcades). So come on, boys: Let's Go With Labour.

**Enter MOTHER and FATHER, very old and frail.**

MOTHER: Who's that?

FATHER: Eh?

MOTHER: There's a man . . .

GEORGE: Do you not recognise me? Aye, well, I suppose I must have changed.

MOTHER: George! It's my own George – oh, here, son, you're lookin' awful well. **(Admires him.)**

FATHER: What have you come for?

GEORGE: What have I come for? – to see *you* of course.

FATHER: Oh, aye . . .

MOTHER: Oh, that's lovely, I knew you'd come back.

GEORGE: And to bring you some news – we're gonnae knock your house down –

FATHER: You're gonnae what?

GEORGE: But first, we're gonnae do it up. Would you like that?

MOTHER: Oh, aye, I suppose we would.

GEORGE: Right, sign here, you can pay in instalments. **(Shouts.)** Right, lads – in here – shift yourselves.

**Enter BUILDERS, who transform the set under GEORGE's supervision – modern sink, TV set, new chairs, dining recess, new purple nylon curtains, new wallpaper, etc. MOTHER and**

**FATHER watch, amazed, appalled. At the end they all look at it. Finally, they turn FATHER's head to the TV.**

GEORGE: Right, lads, every house in the close and every close in the street, then you can get your dinner. **(They go.)**

MOTHER: Here, George, don't you get upset – that's very nice.

GEORGE: It's for you, Mother – it's what Jimmy Maxton, John Wheatley, John MacLean – my forebears in the Labour movement was dreaming of for the working classes. Did you sign that paper?

MOTHER: Aye.

GEORGE: Right, well – I must go now – Mulrinauld (New Towns) Ltd is startin' up in a year or two – I'm away to look at a few fields on the road to Stirling – so I'll be seein' you – and don't forget to pay your rates. **(Goes.)**

MOTHER: It's very nice, very nice.

OLD HEN: **(To YOUNG HEN)** And that is how what is now known as socialism finally came to the Clyde.

## Enter Scotland's oil

OLD HEN: There you are, my girl, that's my story – I saw Scotland on the move, hen – it began with hundreds of thousands of people on the streets of Glasgow singing the *Red Flag*, demanding socialism. It ended wi' this shemozzle we've got now – a string of Labour governments doing the Tories' job for them, and the TUC doing the bosses' job for them: one and a quarter million people out of work. And Glasgow? . . . well . . . that's my story.

YOUNG HEN: Here, Gran, that's a terrible story, so it is – but do you no' think you've left out a few bits ?

OLD HEN: The bits I've left out would keep you here a' night – how that Labour government of Attlee's sold its soul for a few million dollars of Marshall Aid – and if I got on tae Harold Wilson and Reginald Prentice: in the name of –

YOUNG HEN: No, no, no, I was meaning the good bits – I mean folks *do* have better houses and mair food in their belly, and better dole money and better wages now than they used to . . .

OLD HEN: Oh aye, after the war we got quite a lot started. There's a wee bit to show for a' these years, batterin' away. I should bloody hope so. But do you remember Jimmy Maxton? John Wheatley? Willie Gallacher? What they stood for? Do you remember John MacLean – what he died for? No' a few bob here and a high-rise flat there, hen – no: never that – surely we're no' gonnae be satisfied with that – it's *life* we're talking about: how everybody can make the most of the short short time they've got to live. No' just a few people – everybody. That's what socialism's about.

YOUNG HEN: That's what we all want, Gran –

OLD HEN: Aye, but do we all *fight* for it? Do we know *how* to fight for it? Do we have the weapons – organisation and discipline? Or the ammunition – words – and action? Do we *think*? Do we learn? Do we dae anything at all for what we want? Thank Christ *some* do – but where's the others?

YOUNG HEN: You did your bit, eh, Gran?

OLD HEN: Ach, I wasnae anything special, there wis thousands like me – I did what I could, and it wasnae much. It wasnae enough, and I'm still waving a solitary red flag on the number nine bus! And I'm still handin' out bloody pamphlets – here – there's gonnae be a big rally to get that Shrewsbury picket out of gaol – and we *will*, too.

YOUNG HEN: Are you no' gettin' just a wee bit cynical?

OLD HEN: No I am not. I'm busy and I'm waitin'. For you lot to
*see*. And to dae something better –

YOUNG HEN: Us? Christ, you've near put me off altogether . . .

OLD HEN: Are you talkin' about givin' up? Never. You haven't
even started yet. Now – what I'm wantin' to know from you
is – just what do you propose to do that's any different?

YOUNG HEN: Me?

OLD HEN: Aye, you – and that so-called political party of yours
– the Bay City Rollers of Westminster –

YOUNG HEN: Don't you say one word against the Bay City
Rollers – they may be bourgeois pigs, but they're loved.

**Lighting change. Screams (on tape) from speakers. A POP-
GROUP rush on with cut-out guitars, drums, mike. Nod to
tape-operator. Music blasts out. They mime to it, out of sync.**

GROUP: *You see our smiles in the papers*
*The fans all scream and swoon*
*You see us holdin' a cardboard guitar*
*Somebody else plays the tune.*

**Drum break. Three SNP POLITICIANS come on and try to join
in the trendy merry-making.**

GROUP: *It's a revelation*
*The way we wear our jeans –*

SNP POLITICIANS: *It's a revolution*
*Since we came on the scene –*

ALL: *And we're laughin' all the way to the bank*
  *For though we know we're just ornamental*
  *Nothing more than a monumental – prank –*
  *To be frank . . .*
  *We're the craze,*
  *We're the craze,*
  *Nowadays,*
  *We're the craze.*

**Repeat last four lines to fade. GROUP go, leaving three POLITICIANS waving them off. The three SNP politicians are CHARLOTTE SQUARE, an Edinburgh lady enthusiast, HAMISH BANFF, from the North-east, and WILLIAM McCASHIN, an Edinburgh lawyer.**

**MRS CHARLOTTE SQUARE steps forward as GROUP goes, and screams fade.**

MRS CHARLOTTE SQUARE: Wonderful, wonderful. Our boys. So full of vitality, and talent. Now: hello. My name is Mrs Charlotte Square. And I believe that we in the SNP have all of Scotland's ills firmly rooted in our minds. And we are all set to get shot of them altogether.

  Now. Tonight we have two – or should I say 'twa' – speakers, who will, I am sure, make our hearts beat just that little bit faster. So without more ado, I am proud to introduce to you one of our own dear MPs – Mr Hamish Banff.

**She goes and sits, as HAMISH BANFF steps forward, producing typewritten sheet from his pocket, from which he constantly breaks off to give his personal philosophy.**

HAMISH BANFF: Thank you, thank you – er – thank you, Madam Chairman. **(Reads)** 'Greetings, fellow Scots, patriots and sons of Caledonia.' By the way, my name is Hamish Banff, and I'm a couthie wee Nat. Now I have a wee speech here from Party

Headquarters I'd like to read to you – 'Dear Hamish – please stick to the speech' – No, no, that's personal – here it is now – 'Scotland's own dear soil is very precious to me –' oh aye, he's nae telling me naething – I farm eight hundred acres of the best of it – it's no' been a bad year. The bullocks was a bit slow at the beginning but by God they came on at the hinner end. This may have had something to do with the tremendous high price of the barley we kept back from last year's crop. Now I'm not saying we caused prices to fluctuate, but we covered our costs. But keep on complaining, lads. It's the only way to make a spare bob. Now: 'Do not be misled by the propaganda of the London parties – Labour, Liberal or Conservative' – I was a Conservative myself as a matter of fact, stood for parliament for them a few years back; but I soon realised the error of my ways – I didnae get in. Ach, the Tories is done in Scotland. Not patriotic enough. Bloody namby-pamby stuff wi' no grit – nothing but *haute couture* and perfume: I mean Margaret's alright on the floor of the House or in a lobby but could she handle your bullocks – Mind you, she certainly intends to keep a firm grip on the workers – but: let her come to grips with the English workers and leave the Scottish working man to us – Where was I? Oh aye, propaganda – 'do not be mislead by the propaganda of the London parties, we in Scotland are on the road to untold riches' – well, some of us have got untold riches right now, and as long as they remain untold, there'll be no more questions asked. You see – we need the business fraternity as our friends, make no mistake about that – and that is why we've gone to the trouble to set up our Economics Advisory Committee – with your boys from the merchant banks and the investment trusts and the Stock Exchange – to tell us exactly how to run Scotland – and make a profit: no skimping – these are the best men – when it comes to making a bob or two – and after independence that's what we'll all be in it for – er, in for. 'We are going to give Scottish businessmen a fair crack of the whip.' Now I realise that's a dangerous image that, but we're no' sayin' who's back we're cracking it on. I'll say this, though, you won't see the blood for the colour of the shirt.

Aye, and we'll have the labourers back in the bothies singing bothy ballads and snapping up their bowl of brose, that's what made Scotland great, not wasting their time chasing better wages like they do in England. All these realities will become a dream when our own dear Scotia becomes a nation once again. Thank you. **(Sits.)**

## MRS CHARLOTTE SQUARE gets up, applauding.

MRS CHARLOTTE SQUARE: Thank you, Hamish. What a rugged wee Scot you are. Now I'm going to hand you over to a *real thinker*. Scotland's answer to Sir Alec Douglas Home – and all the other great political philosophers of the twentieth century.

I think you're going to appreciate what this man has to offer – I know I do – here he is – a man who needs no introduction . . .

## Sits, as WILLIAM McCASHIN rises to speak.

McCASHIN: Fellow Scots, others. William McCashin speaking. As things looked quite promising for this great movement of ours, I thought I'd better join it. I'm a thinker, and an Edinburgh lawyer. So I'm a pretty quick thinker.

Now many witless people, some having the misfortune to be non-Scottish, have accused us of not having any policies. That's not true. We have. I remember them well. In fact I have them written on the back of this piece of paper. I will put them to you in the form of questions and answers. In that order, question, then answer. Thus you might well ask: What is your policy on housing? You might well ask that. Well, our policy is: After independence there will be housing in Scotland. But it will be Scottish housing – that just about covers that one.

Now, we don't need, as a party, to go into details. It's obvious that, after independence, the details will be worked out.

What – next question – what is your policy on the economy? Answer: After independence, the Scottish economy will boom – But that's not all – no, wait for it – thanks to our oil. I mean – would you rather be Rich and Scottish, or Poor and English? Any fool could answer that one. Several fools have.

I mean, now we've got our oil – well, now the multi-national oil companies have got our oil – there must be a bob or two in it for you and me. Preferably a bob for you and two for me. **(Laughs.)** No, no. Surely the Americans will slip us the odd quid here and there. Now – nationalisation. I say no – the Americans wouldn't like it. So forget about national-isation. After independence – don't offend the Americans, and support Scottish bosses. That's not a policy, by the way, that's just stating the obvious. Next question: Is the SNP a left-wing or a right-wing party? The simple answer to that is yes. And no. We simply think up the policies that are right for Scotland – and that, of course, has nothing to do with politics. Now there are a lot of people, including rank-and-file members of the SNP – even one or two optimistic vice-chairmen, going round saying: 'After independence, Scotland will be socialist'. Now, I don't want to scare you people, but socialism means secret police, massacre of women and children, rape, arson, looting, thuggery, monumental architecture, anarchy, chaos, civil war, American intervention possibly with H-bombs, the death of all we hold near and dear – and workers getting more wages. Now this last one's the real problem. So we've thought of a policy to deal with that. After independence, Scotland will definitely not be a socialist country. Though of course there is still a high level of democratic discussion – in the East Kilbride Branch.

No, we will put an end to dividing Scotsman from fellow Scotsman. After all, Hugh Fraser is just the same, under the kilt, as any common old working chap. And Glasgow belongs to both of them. What do they both want? Money. Well, our New Politics rises above class-wars and divisiveness, and all that out-dated political jargon – and says we must all get together to make money for Hugh Fraser.

That is my glimpse into the future. It appeals to a lot of people in Scotland, and if you'll take my advice, you'll join the party now – and don't forget, the holder of the lucky membership card number drawn out of the bonnet by Billy Wolfe with his eyes shut facing both ways at the same time, could be MP for Moray and Nairn. Thank you.

MRS CHARLOTTE SQUARE: What a man! We will now rise and sing the party song – one, two, three . . . **(One sings *Scots wha hae*, another *Scotland the Brave*, and another *Floor o' Scotland*)**

**After a short cacophony, a moment of confusion, they ALL go, to taped screams, etc. YOUNG HEN comes on, furious.**

YOUNG HEN: Is that how you think we are?

OLD HEN: It's no' so far off . . . some of yous are a sight worse –

YOUNG HEN: Aye, I know, I've got tae admit it – but some of us is a lot better – in my branch we want mair than freedom for Scotland – we want social justice.

OLD HEN: Social justice? What the hell kind of a Tory expression is that?

YOUNG HEN: Tory?

OLD HEN: How can you have social justice without economic justice? – and how can you have economic justice without socialism? You know fine what I'm sayin' . . .

YOUNG HEN: But some of us *are* socialists.

OLD HEN: Aye, so you say – but where *are* ye? Let's hear from you.

YOUNG HEN: The first thing we've got to do is get Scotland *free*, then you'll see where the socialists are.

OLD HEN: Do you no think that might be a wee bit late? Let's be hearing from you *now*, before your bankers and your think-tank and your failed Tories take you over completely.

YOUNG HEN: Aye, but first we must get independence, so we've got to stay united. After independence . . .

OLD HEN: Oh God. Here we go again – do you no see what I'm sayin' to you? Now come on – for it matters, girl: what are you gonnae dae any different from us? You're gonnae move your parliament from London to Edinburgh, but it's gonnae still be there tae keep the people quiet and under the thumb – what difference is any of that gonnae make? None at all. And your precious oil – look – there's not one man – or woman – in your party gonnae make that much impact on the multinational corporations – all you'd be gettin' after independence is a few people grabbin' a bigger slice of the same bloody capitalist cake – Come on, girl – I'm waiting for you tae speak.

YOUNG HEN: Aye, well, I cannae get a word in edgeways –

OLD HEN: Well try to avoid stupid expressions like social justice – you lot don't *read* enough, you use words that don't mean anythin'. You've learnt nothin' from two hundred years of working-class history. All you can do is – Scotland! Well, don't forget, *I'm* for a free Scotland: free of England, aye, but free of capitalist greed, misery and exploitation – right. Go.

YOUNG HEN: Well. I don't know. It's just we stand mair chance on our own . . .

OLD HEN: True, true.

YOUNG HEN: And we believe in democracy – I know that – and participation.

OLD HEN: Participation? What's that mean? Put the unions on the board wi' the bosses? An old capitalist trick tae con the workers – nothing more nor less –

YOUNG HEN: Gran, can I finish?

OLD HEN: Aye, but you'll need to do better than that.

YOUNG HEN: Ah, hell, Gran – can you no see – it's an emotional thing – it's pride, the pride of a whole nation that wants to be free.

OLD HEN: Aye, I know . . . I feel it myself – But, but, *but*.

YOUNG HEN: And Scotland's on the move – right now.

OLD HEN: And so were we – but do you no' see the mistake we made: we put politics – that's Westminster and government, up here, and it failed us. Then we put economics – that's unions and General Strikes and abolition of capitalism, up here – and it failed us: why? Because the two must go together. When the working-class of Scotland gets itself on the move, and organised, for both together – *then* you'll see something. That's what you should be fighting for.

YOUNG HEN: I'll need tae think about that –

OLD HEN: So you will. Here, I'm away now, to get these pamphlets out – imagine that lad in prison still for defending his pals against MacAlpine's thugs. **(Gives her a pamphlet.)** Here, it's just like nineteen twenty-six all over again – now come in and see me when you can – don't forget – I enjoy a wee blether with you, girl. It's true, she's a good girl: Cheery-bye now. **(Goes.)**

**YOUNG HEN looks at pamphlet then looks up wondering. OTHERS come on as themselves, repeating lines they have acted before.**

MOTHER: Alright, so when wee Agnes died, me and your father moved in here and Henrietta on the floor and you got the room to yourself – bloody lucky you were, too . . .

FATHER: Meetin', votin'? Here, don't waste your good pamphlets on me: I don't vote, nor do I go to meetin's . . .

GEORGE: I'm fed up being a working-class fool.

CHARLIE: You'll no get anything without a bit of trouble, Freddie.

**KING GEORGE V appears at the back of the stage in his robes.**

KING GEORGE V: We suppose we might as well let them play at being Prime Ministers and Home Secretaries and that sort of thing. As far as we can see it won't make any difference to anything serious: our City owns all our money. Our industialists own our industries, our Church owns the minds of our people – we have our Army, our Navy, our Air Force and our police constables to see to that. **(Goes.)**

MAXTON: I could ask no greater job in life than to make English-ridden, capitalist-ridden, landowner-ridden Scotland into the Scottish Socialist Commonwealth – and in doing that, I'd be doing a great service to the people of England, Wales and the world.

GALLACHER: I believe there is only one way for the working people of this country to end the exploitation of their labour and their lives, and that is to seize state power, retain it, and establish the dictatorship of the proletariat as a means of transition to a communist society.

WHEATLEY: At the present moment workers' representatives are powerless in the House of Commons. All our eggs must not be found in the parliamentary basket.

MAXTON: In the end you find you have built not the Palace of Socialist Freedom, but a slum dwelling for, the working-class.

MacLEAN: The day of social pottering or reform is past. However Labour may attain power, it must get full possession of the land and all means of production in order to use these co-operatively by the whole community for the benefit of all.

SINGER: **(sings)** *Little Hen gives all her strength to win that fight,*
*Seems her strength is never done;*
*Little Hen gives all she has, she knows she's right –*
*Nothing's going to stop her, till the fight is won.*

**Beat of music changes. Lights change. SINGER turns to audience. The rest of COMPANY join in as the last song progresses:**

*You working folk of Scotland,*
*All you who want her free*
*Remember John MacLean right well*
*Or free you'll never be.*

*What freedom you call*
*Is not freedom at all*
*Till tyranny is done*
*Not England alone but the tyrants at home*
*Must go before we've won.*

*What good's your flags and banners*
*What good's your Bannockburn*
*When Scotland's full of money-men*
*Who'll rob you in their turn.*

*What freedom you call, etc.*

*We'll proudly build a Scotland*
*Where landlords' fences fall*
*Whose industry's for you and me*
*Where each can work for all.*

*What freedom you call, etc.*

*You working folk of Scotland*
*All you who want her free*
*Remember John MacLean right well*
*Or free you'll never be.*

**At end of song, black-out.**

# End of Play

# Historical Note on the 7:84 Theatre Company

The 7:84 Theatre Company was formed in 1971 by John McGrath, Elizabeth MacLennan and a few like-minded theatre makers. The name was taken from a statistic in *The Economist* that 7% of the population of the UK owned 84% of the wealth. Things have not improved greatly. They toured extensively in Scotland, England and Wales. Early productions were *Trees in the Wind* by John McGrath, *The Ballygombeen Bequest* by John Arden and Margaretta D'Arcy, *Serjeant Musgrave Dances On* adapted by John McGrath and *Occupations* by Trevor Griffiths. The Company divided in two in 1973 to form a company in Scotland and one based in England. They continued to tour throughout the UK and in Europe and Canada, until the funding for 7:84 England was cut by the Arts Council in 1984.

The Scottish Company's first show was *The Cheviot the Stag and the Black Black Oil* by John McGrath. It toured all round the Highlands and Islands in village halls and community centres, and met with a tremendous reception. The BBC made a version for its Play for Today series. After this the Company did *The Game's a Bogey* by John McGrath, about the Glasgow socialist John McLean. This play was in the style of a variety show, and toured technical colleges, miner's clubs, trades councils, universities, town halls and civic centres in the Lowlands. Between them, the companies presented over fifty new plays until John McGrath resigned as Artistic Director of 7:84 Scotland in 1988.

John wrote in the original programme notes to *Out of Our Heads*:

**'There are now two different kinds of theatre – different not necessarily in subject-matter, or even in style, but different in their attitudes to style and subject, and different in the audiences they are seeking to entertain.**

One kind of theatre is dedicated to its patrons, the mainly middle-class theatre goers. It presents them with a varied fare of plays – the great classics of the past, or new plays which will confirm the values of that audience about life today. Occasionally it will question those values, provide those audiences with 'food for thought'. The working class, when it appears in this kind of theatre, is an alien object, to be explained, patronised, with sentimentality or laughed at. Very rarely to be taken seriously.

The other kind of theatre, which 7:84 did a great deal to establish, is there to present the realities of working class life and history directly to working class audiences. Without translating it into the language of the middle class 'theatre' that has dominated our stages since the 1890s. It has its roots in the popular tradition of entertainment, and it takes the values of the working class very seriously.

With the Scottish 7:84 Theatre Company, we put on shows about the history of the people of the Highlands from the time of the Clearances to present day; about John MacLean, the great pioneer socialist; about the twin pressures on Highland people today of the land-ownership situation and the oil boom; about the great days of Red Clyde and the new aspirations of the SNP; about the history of the people of Dumbarton; about the presence of the USA and its role in Scotland; about the lives of ordinary people in industrial areas; about the need for a Scottish Parliament and about sexism and ageism. We used forms of entertainment that audiences are familiar with; the ceilidh, the variety show, the concert party, music hall, band shows, the musical play. These were used as the basis from which different styles and techniques emerged and were developed as forms of theatre.

Our audiences were found in village halls, community centres, town halls, technical colleges, miners' clubs, trades council clubs, civic centres, even an auction room as well as in theatres.

Inevitably we talked about politics because it is a reality of life today and because theatre is about the way people relate to each other – and that is conditioned by economic structures, from which spring social structures, like classes and cultural patterns; like educational systems, religion and the customary relationship between the sexes. Any theatre that concentrates on 'emotional' plots and does not question the structure that underlie its characters' lives is being political by default. We chose to examine political issues openly because they shape the reality we all live in. Than reality is not static and accepted – it is dynamic and in the process of change. If it is to change in a way that will make living better, then an open, clear analysis is needed. We hope that our kind of theatre can make a contribution to the way people decide their own future – and on the way give people some good theatre, some enjoyable music, a few laughs and a good night out.'

Many of the writers and performers who worked with 7:84 went on to form their own highly esteemed companies – notably Belt and Braces, Monstrous Regiment, The Project Theatre Dublin, Headlines Theatre Vancouver and Wildcat. John McGrath's work has influenced many young theatre makers. His plays continue to be regarded as challenging and innovative in style, content and entertainment value.

**Elizabeth MacLennan 2008**

# Chronology of Plays
## by John McGrath

| Year | Title | Company/Theatre (first production) |
|---|---|---|
| 1958 | *A Man Has Two Fathers* (a play in two acts) | Oxford University Drama Society |
| 1958 | *The Tent* (a one-act play) | Royal Court, London |
| 1959 | *Why the Chicken?* (a play in two acts) | Oxford University Theatre Group |
| 1960 | *Tell Me, Tell Me* (short sketch) | Live New Departures Institute of Contemporary Arts |
| 1960 | *Take It* (short sketch) | Live New Departures Institute of Contemporary Arts |
| 1960 | *Jack* (a play with songs) (music by Dudley Moore) | Unperformed |
| 1963 | *Basement in Bangkok* (a play with songs) (music by Dudley Moore) | Student Group, Bristol |
| 1966 | *Events While Guarding the Bofors Gun* (a play in two acts) | Hampstead Theatre |
| 1968 | *Bakke's Night of Fame* (an adaptation based on William Butler's novel *The Danish Gambit*) | Hampstead Theatre |
| 1969 | *Comrade Jacob* (an adaptation based on the novel by David Caute) | Gardner Arts Centre |

| | | |
|---|---|---|
| 1970 | *Random Happenings in the Hebrides* (a play in two acts) | Edinburgh Lyceum Edinburgh International Festival |
| 1970 | *Sharpeville Crackers* (a multi-media collage) | Lyceum Theatre, London |
| 1971 | *Unruly Elements* (six one-act plays) (renamed *Plugged Into History*) | Liverpool Everyman |
| 1971 | *Trees in the Wind* (a play with songs) | 7:84 |
| 1971 | *Soft or a Girl* (a rock musical) (renamed *My Pal and Me*) | Liverpool Everyman |
| 1972 | *Plugged into History* (six one-act plays) | 7:84 |
| 1972 | *Out of Sight* (a one-act play) | 7:84 |
| 1972 | *Underneath* (a play with songs) | 7:84 |
| 1972 | *Serjeant Musgrave Dances On* (an adaptation based on John Arden's *Serjeant Musgrave's Dance*) | 7:84 |
| 1972 | *Fish in the Sea* (a play with music) | Liverpool Everyman |
| 1973 | *The Cheviot, the Stag and the Black, Black Oil* (a ceilidh play) | 7:84 Scotland |
| 1974 | *The Game's a Bogey* (a variety show) | 7:84 Scotland |

| 1974 | *Boom*<br>(a musical play) | 7:84 Scotland |
|------|----|----|
| 1975 | *My Pal and Me*<br>(a rock musical) | 7:84 Scotland |
| 1975 | *Lay Off*<br>(a play with songs) | 7:84 England |
| 1975 | *Little Red Hen*<br>(a play with music) | 7:84 Scotland |
| 1975 | *Yobbo Nowt*<br>(a musical play) | 7:84 England |
| 1975 | *Oranges and Lemons*<br>(a one-act play) | Amsterdam Theatre<br>Festival |
| 1976 | *Out of Our Heads*<br>(a play with songs) | 7:84 Scotland |
| 1976 | *The Rat Trap*<br>(a political allegory with songs) | 7:84 England |
| 1977 | *Trembling Giant*<br>(a pantomime for children<br>of all ages, with songs) | 7:84 England<br>and 7:84 Scotland |
| 1977 | *Joe of England*<br>(a play with songs) | 7:84 England |
| 1979 | *Joe's Drum*<br>(a play with songs) | 7:84 Scotland |
| 1979 | *Big Square Fields*<br>(a play with songs) | 7:84 England |
| 1979 | *Bitter Apples*<br>(a musical) | 7:84 England |
| 1979 | *If You Want to*<br>*Know the Time* (satire) | Blair Peach Memorial Event,<br>Royal Court |

| | | |
|---|---|---|
| 1980 | *Swings and Roundabouts* (a comedy with songs) | 7:84 Scotland |
| 1980 | *Blood Red Roses* (a play with songs) | 7:84 Scotland |
| 1981 | *The Catch or Red Herrings in the Minch* (a play with songs) | 7:84 Scotland |
| 1981 | *Nightclass* (a play with songs) | 7:84 England |
| 1982 | *Rejoice!* (a play with songs) | 7:84 England |
| 1983 | *On the Pig's Back* (street theatre) (written with David MacLennan) | 7:84 Scotland/Wildcat |
| 1983 | *The Woman of the Dunes* (a community play) | Ijmuiden, Holland |
| 1983 | *Women in Power* (a musical play) (adapted from *Thesmophoriazusae* by Aristophanes) | General Gathering Edinburgh International Festival |
| 1984 | *The Baby and the Bathwater* (a one-person play with music) | 7:84 Scotland |
| 1984 | *Six Men of Dorset* (a documentary play) (adapted from the play by Miles Malleson and Harry Brooks) | 7:84 England |
| 1985 | *The Albannach* (a play with songs) (adapted from the novel by Fionn MacColla) | 7:84 Scotland |

| 1985 | *All the Fun of the Fair* (carnival theatre) | 7:84 England |
|------|----|----|
| 1986 | *There is a Happy Land* (a concert on the entire history of the Gaels) | 7:84 Scotland |
| 1987 | *Mairi Mhor –* *the Woman from Skye* (a play with songs) | 7:84 Scotland |
| 1989 | *Border Warfare* (an historical pageant with songs) | Wildcat/Freeway Films |
| 1990 | *John Brown's Body* (an historical pageant with songs) | Wildcat/Freeway Films |
| 1992 | *The Wicked Old Man* (a black comedy) | West Yorkshire Playhouse |
| 1992 | *Watching for Dolphins* (a one-person play) | Freeway Stage |
| 1994 | *The Silver Darlings* (an adaptation based on the novel by Neil Gunn) | Wildcat |
| 1994 | *Half the Picture* (a documentary play written with Richard Norton Taylor) | Tricycle Theatre |
| 1994 | *Reading Rigoberta* (a one-person play) | Freeway Stage |
| 1996 | *The Last of the MacEachans* (a one-person comedy) | Freeway Stage |
| 1996 | *A Satire of the Fourth Estaite* (a satire based on Sir David Lindsay's *Ane Satyre of the Thrie Estaitis*) | Wildcat |

| 1996 | *Media Star* (a play for schools) | Theatre Workshop, Edinburgh |
| 1997 | *Worksong* (a play for schools) | TAG [Theatre About Glasgow] |
| 2000 | *The Road to Mandalay* (a musical play for schools) | Bryn Celynnog School, Pontypridd |
| 2001 | *HyperLynx* (a one-person play) | Floodtide |

# Writings on the Theatre

*A Good Night Out*, Nick Hern Books 1996.

*The Bone Won't Break*, Methuen 1990.

*Naked Thoughts*, Nick Hern Books 2002.